Mars in Aries

Studies in Austrian Literature, Culture, and Thought

Translation Series

Alexander Lernet-Holenia

Mars in Aries

Translated by
Robert von Dassanowsky and
Elisabeth Littell Frech

Afterword by
Robert von Dassanowsky

ARIADNE PRESS
Riverside, California

Ariadne Press would like to express its appreciation to the Bundeskanzleramt - Sektion Kunst, Vienna for assistance in publishing this book.

.KUNST

Translated from the German
Mars im Widder
© Paul Zsolnay Verlag, Wien 1976, 1997

Library of Congress Cataloging-in-Publication Data

Lernet-Holenia, Alexander, 1897-1976.
    [Mars im Widder. English]
    Mars in Aries / Alexander Lernet-Holenia ; translated by Robert von Dassanowsky and Elisabeth Littell Frech ; afterword by Robert von Dassanowsky.
        p.   cm. -- (Studies in Austrian literature, culture and thought. Translation series)
    ISBN 1-57241-118-X
    I. Dassanowsky, Robert. II. Frech, Elisabeth Littell. III. Title. IV. Series.

PT2623.E74 M3413 2003
833'.912--dc21   2002028209

Cover Design:
Art Director: George McGinnis
Design and Photography: Matthew Richardson

Foreword to the 1947 Edition of *Mars im Widder*

The novel *Mars im Widder* was written between December 15, 1939 and February 15, 1940. Shortly thereafter, under the auspices of my friends Paul Wiegler and L. E. Reindl, it appeared before its official publication, in a magazine of the German Publishers. The preprint drew so much attention, not only in Germany, but also with the troops in the field (if in fact it was read the way I meant it to be) that the 15,000 copies of the book that were produced in Leipzig for S. Fischer Publishers in the spring of 1941 were banned by the Propaganda Ministry and the Wehrmacht. The entire edition was hidden, but then burned during the attacks on Leipzig in winter 1943/1944. One single copy in my possession was preserved. Using it as a model, with only a few minor stylistic improvements, the text is now being republished.

Alexander Lernet-Holenia

Acknowledgment

The translators wish to thank
Alexander Dreihann-Holenia and Jorun B. Johns
for their encouragement;
Richard H. Lawson and Martha Morris Frech
for their generous advice.

1

At the start of summer 1939, the principal character – if not to say the hero – of this truthful report, a certain Wallmoden, resolved to begin a mandatory military maneuver on August 15. But it would have been difficult for him to tell why he had chosen this point in time rather than any other. For it would have been left to him to make up his mind – quite as well, or even rather – in favor of September 1 – which would have eventually made a great difference; but no one would have objected if he had, for instance, reported on September 15 or even only on October 1. But, as has been stated, he already appeared at his regiment on August 15. Later he explained that he had simply worked this date out. But how he had worked it out, he could not say. He was only able to state that he had the feeling of having been expected there and then. But by whom? The regiment certainly did not await him. No one knew him there yet, and even without him the service would certainly not have been delayed.

Perhaps his preparations or calculations had been of a different sort entirely – and perhaps life in general only continues because it is based on such similar, but in any case completely unconscious, decisions. For if human beings were merely dependent on the power of their understanding, they would apparently not even reach the age at which it would be possible for them to employ their understanding. Admittedly, some people claim that one's way of life is merely dependent on one's own will and that all other views could be nothing else but fantasy. But there are also those who will only admit that the lot of the living is cast by none other than fate. It is probable that every existence is simply dependent on both. And yet, the two realms of power, that of will and that of fate, are incongruent. They never overlap completely. Only one thing is certain: that these spheres work into each other and that fate serves will and, ultimately, will only serves fate – of which the following might be an example.

Already as Wallmoden was making preparations to leave his house, he thought he had felt that this particular departure would be one of great import. Certainly, human sensitivity for a beloved, or for things, is bound to the fear of loss. One always leaves a loved one or a home, so that at the moment of a true departure, the farewell is already so well prepared that it almost seems easy. Wallmoden, however, did not find this departure from home at all easy, and suffered from the unclear and even unfathomable feelings that this departure conjured up. Yes, these were the first of many repetitious and increasing feelings to come – which were as if he had been caught up in the gears of events by the seam or the hem of his clothing, and which continued to pull him in and would from now on manipulate his movements... For instance, if he stood at the window and looked into the garden, he felt this garden had finished with him and rustled its indifference under the cloudy sky for someone else. And as he walked through the rooms, the sight of the pictures of the persons he descended from did not reassure him. Instead, they gazed back at him rather mockingly, with raised eyebrow, as if they could not understand his mood and the reasons for a distress they had never known. Go, they seemed to say, just go! If you do not leave, then you cannot return. During his last nights at home, he was forced to admit to himself that his disposition had really begun to waver in this unusual manner, as he wandered through the house with candlelight (he had no idea why). The hunting trophies on the top floor gave him the impression that along with the giant shadows of the fourteen- and sixteen-antler branch mountings, there was also a flock of shadowy people who fled from one side of the hall to the other, as if they were game escaping through the thickets.

He had already become a witness and participant to a bizarre conversation among the officers on his first day at the regiment.

This discussion began with a story by First Lieutenant Mauritz, who led the engineers' troops: a young man from the city, the son of a baker, had drowned while swimming in the river. For two days they searched for his body but it could not be found.

That it was even possible for a man to drown in such a relatively shallow river was for Mauritz as fictional as the banishment of bad luck, which was accorded this event.

After some discussion about the various methods used to find the body – poles, nets, and such – and about the opaque quality of the river's water, Lieutenant Obentraut suggested that the best method to locate the drowned man would be a seance in which the spirit of the victim would be conjured up and could then be asked as to the location of the corpse.

At first, this was generally understood to be a joke, which one might make in such intimate company in order to end a pointless conversation. After some time, everyone was surprised to discover that Obentraut was not without interest in carrying through this suggested experiment. Despite his youth, the Lieutenant was a very retiring sort who rarely joined his comrades in their nightly social doings, preferring instead to devote himself to the intellectual perusal of countless books, which probably accounted for his unique views on God and the world.

Even more surprising was that the usually neutral Major

Baron Dombaste did not completely dismiss the views of Lieutenant Obentraut out of hand. The Major stated that he did not believe it possible to summon the dead, but that it was without question possible to summon the living. He told the following tale:

"One of my cousins had long been in love with a young Russian woman, whom I shall call Nadja. But this great love, which was mutual and even overwhelming, was to end tragically. It was precisely *because* their passions were so far beyond normal feelings that the Russian woman left my cousin, even imagining that he had deceived her. Maybe he had in fact deceived her. But perhaps even more important, his actions may have been nothing other than an escape, as were hers.

"It was said that Nadja had gone to Constantinople and died soon after. At least so we believed. One evening during the autumn hunting season at my cousin's house, we got the idea of holding a seance. There was no specific spirit that we wanted to call. But probably because my cousin had so intensively thought about his lost love during all of this, an invisible presence made itself known through tapping signals and called itself Nadja.

"Deeply upset, my cousin interrupted the seance immediately.

"A few days later, one of his guests could not sleep and decided to fetch a book from the library. To his astonishment he found a young lady there, whom he did not know and whom he had never noticed at the house.

"She was very beautiful, and he entertained himself with her for about a quarter of an hour, after which she rose and left the room through a hidden door he had not seen before.

"'Who was the young lady in the library last night?' he asked my cousin the next morning.

"'What young lady?' said my cousin, to which the other attempted a description. 'She looked so and so,' he said; 'she spoke in a most enchanting way, and when she smiled, one saw the most beautiful teeth. There was only one small irregularity, next to the left incisor, as if a tooth hadn't grown out properly when she was a child. But this made her smile even more attractive.'

"My cousin went white as a ghost. After this description he believed that there was no question that it was Nadja's spirit they had conjured up and which was now haunting the vicinity.

"A few nights later everyone was awakened by the cracks of several shots. My cousin was found in his bedroom, lying wounded in his blood, and leaning over him was Nadja beside herself with tears. She had intended to kill him and then herself.

"It had not been Nadja's ghost, but Nadja in flesh and blood who had fired the shots. Obviously no power on earth could have conjured her spirit, since she had only pretended to be dead in order to escape the unbearable relationship with my cousin. His thoughts of her were enough to call back the *living*. She had followed a sudden, completely inexplicable force from abroad, and wanted to finally end her unhappy passion in death with my cousin.

"But the shots did not kill and were like the fulfillment of thunder in the tension of stormy air. Both of them, Nadja and my cousin, have been happily married for many years."

This story satisfied everyone by its rational conclusion. But Wallmoden commented: "Stories which are neither completely spiritual or completely normal are the most interesting after all."

"Why do you believe this?" asked the Cavalry Captain von Sodoma.

"Because our entire life also takes place in such a twilight realm," said Wallmoden. "For example, it is said that my great-grandfather had a very strange experience, which cannot be described as either supernatural nor natural."

"And what sort of experience was it?" asked Sodoma.

"He was a colonel – in command of a regiment," said

8

Wallmoden. "A few days before the Battle of Santa Lucia, in which he commanded an army corps, he decided to inspect his regiment. But he did not wish himself announced. He was therefore all the more surprised that the regiment was already awaiting him at attention when he arrived with his staff. The armored cavalry, two rows deep, were in a motionless line, straighter than a ray of sunshine. Their white coats were spotless; every cord shined, no buttons missing, and at the helm, every standard displayed oak leaves, despite their scarcity in this region.

"He immediately asked the reporting Lieutenant Colonel how they knew he was coming.

"The Lieutenant Colonel answered: 'Your excellency had announced his presence.'"

"'Announced?' my grandfather exclaimed. 'Through whom?'

"'Personally, of course!' replied the Lieutenant Colonel, and the commander had the opportunity to study a perplexed face – his own – peering from under a helmet of parrot-green feathers in the splendidly sparkling copper neck shield on the guard uniform of his subordinate, as if he were looking into a shaving mirror.

"He had already surmised that an indiscreet member of his staff had communicated subrosa with the regiment. But after a long interrogation, he could no longer doubt that two hours earlier, he had ridden into the camp alone and had called out to the guard: 'Boys, I will be inspecting the regiment at four o'clock. I don't wish to be disappointed!'

"Everyone had been amazed to see him arrive without accompaniment. Yet during this supposed ride through camp, he had in actuality just finished eating and was napping for a few minutes in his tent. He could not recall if he had dreamed he was riding through the camp."

"Thank goodness for such superiors," said First Lieutenant Mauritz.

"And did he have other experiences like this?" asked Major Dombaste.

"Nothing else has been passed down," said Wallmoden. "But after this, his soldiers were convinced that he could spirit about anywhere."

"Well, that's good!" laughed Sodoma. "That somebody doesn't even know if he is spiriting is actually very good! I, however, believe that this could not happen to me against my will, and I declare myself ready to inform you immediately if I should spirit about."

The Lieutenant Obentraut gazed at him with his thoughtfully owlish eyes and said: "Perhaps Cavalry Captain will be able to -perhaps not."

"Why not?" insisted Sodoma.

"Because we are not even certain if we know when we are dead. I have read, for example, that a man lost consciousness in a street accident. When he came to, he found himself lying in his bed, surrounded by all his friends who had died some time ago.

"'What are you doing here?' he asked them. 'You are all dead!'

"'You as well,' said one of them."

Sodoma didn't quite know how to reply to this. Finally he said: "This is becoming ever more confusing! Firstly, Wallmoden's grandfather, or great-grandfather, or whatever he may have been, was not yet dead when he was spiriting. And secondly, if the two people you spoke of were really dead, then how does the world know about this illuminating conversation between two ghosts?"

Obentraut shrugged his shoulders and said: "Well, the Cavalry Captain will see."

"What will I see?" bellowed Sodoma. "I will see nothing! - And as far as you are concerned," he turned to Wallmoden, "I will from here on out consider it my sworn duty to clearly inform you if it is me or my spirit which you will have the pleasure of greeting."

"Very kind of you!" said Wallmoden, who had no idea what else to say.

2

On this day, a Tuesday, near evening, Wallmoden requested a few hours leave to drive to Vienna. Sodoma, who was also on his way there, offered him a ride. The drive lasted about one hour from the garrison where the regiment was stationed.

"Come up for a bit," said Sodoma when they arrived. "My wife is here too. She is staying with her parents for a few days."

As they entered the Sodomas' apartment, they found Frau von Sodoma in the company of a lady neither recognized. For some reason she reminded Wallmoden of the Russian girl in the story Major Dombaste told after dinner: Nadja, who was believed to be dead and whom the Major's cousin had nearly shot. The Major had not described her in his tale, but Wallmoden would swear that she could only look like this woman. He had begun to confuse what was told and what he experienced. Indeed, his impression was so strong that as he was introduced to the young woman, who smiled at him for a brief moment, he attempted to find the small irregularity in her teeth, which Dombaste had mentioned in his story. But her teeth shimmered like a choice strand of pearls. Even if she was not French or Spanish, one could assume French or Spanish extraction. Her poise, above all, the way she carried herself, was uncommonly fine, and she had an exquisite hairline, which was blond. The rest of her hair, which had a matte shine, was dark brown to black. She wore it relatively high and pulled toward the back, similar to the hairstyles of French ladies in the time before the Great Revolution. Her eyes were both dark and light; blue rays encircled her pupils and she had long, curled lashes. There was the slightest suggestion of a shadow on her cheeks.

Her mouth did not fit her face. It was a bit too wide, almost ordinary. Nevertheless, Wallmoden found it to be "ordinary in a most stimulating manner." It expressed passion, but at the same time offered traces of playfulness around the edges, as if it were amused by its own temperament.

"Who is this?" Wallmoden asked Sodoma in a half-whisper, while the women continued their conversation interrupted by their arrival.

Sodoma replied that he had no idea, but then did answer Wallmoden's question sometime later as they were leaving and after he had exchanged a few words with his wife: she is Baroness Pistohlkors – his wife had only met her yesterday in the company of some friends.

Pistohlkors spoke almost exclusively with Frau von Sodoma, and continuously glanced at the men with something like curious surprise, if one of them should make a comment. For example, when the Cavalry Captain inquired about his children, whom he had not seen for some days, he was thrown a punishing stare in response. This sort of entertainment was hardly pleasant for either Sodoma or Wallmoden. Both remained, it seemed, only to finish their cigarettes. Sodoma poured his guest and himself repeated shots of schnapps from a flask into wide glasses while Pistohlkors continued to act as if the men were nonexistent until she finally rose and with a sigh, as if her meeting with Frau von Sodoma had been hopelessly disturbed, declared she must leave. Wallmoden took this opportunity to escape.

He had escorted her to the stairs, so he asked her, for the sake of good manners, if he might drop her somewhere by car. She immediately gave him an address in the Silesianergasse. During the ride, she was completely different than at the Sodomas. Above all, she no longer pretended to be surprised when spoken to – prompting Wallmoden to ask, as she stepped out of the car, if he might see her again.

"When?" she quizzed, after a pause.

"Tonight would be best," he replied.

She told him that would not be possible. He wanted to know why. She was busy. He asked her what would take up her time. Acquaintances had entrusted a letter to her, she said. They had asked her to deliver it to a particular address – tonight.

That is hardly a reason, he explained, to keep them from meeting later. Delivering a letter would not take long. In fact, he would make himself available for the task. In the meantime, she could change. Where was the letter to be delivered?

She gave his uniform a worried look. He had expected that she would name some distant address, somewhere in Rodaun or Heiligenstadt, but she told him to deliver the letter to an address in the Piaristengasse.

"The Piaristengasse?" he exclaimed. "That's only a few minutes from here."

"I would ask you to please not come by for me before eight o'clock. It will take me that long to change."

"May I have the letter?" She pulled it out of her bag. It was rather large, sealed and without address.

"Will you be able to remember the address?" she asked.

"Certainly."

"Until eight then," she replied after another odd pause.

"Until eight."

It was now a few minutes after seven. It had started to become dusk, and a street lantern threw a flickering gaslight onto the irregular pavement. A wind had gusted through the street, which caused the flame to flicker. A shutter on an open window of one of the houses battered and a branch of an oak, hanging over a high wall, rustled. The sky encased the darkening city like some strange cathedral dome made of transparent emerald. In the direction of the Strohgasse, which crossed the Salesianergasse, a single red star appeared like a lance tip of polished copper.

Wallmoden's eyes followed the young woman as she walked into the entrance of her building. He noticed that she had unusually beautiful legs, and he recalled the saying of a friend: one must never begin anything with a woman who has really attractive legs. If a woman has a beautiful face, she might still moderate its effect. But if she has beautiful legs, she can not help but be aware of their effect and will use this to her advantage.

A servant opened the door to the house at the address to which Pistohlkors had directed him in the Piaristengasse. Wallmoden handed him the letter and turned to leave when the servant requested that he enter and wait a moment.

Wallmoden, who had no idea why he even should be here, stepped into the foyer, and the servant, carrying the letter on a platter, disappeared through one of the room's many doors. For a brief time Wallmoden was alone. He had no idea whose home this was. The entry door offered no name plaque. The doors of the foyer were covered in green cloth and the room was decorated with a few hunting articles and trophies.

The apartment was on the second floor of the building.

After a few minutes, the servant reappeared and asked Wallmoden to follow him. In the room that they entered, he saw an attractive, perhaps somewhat haggard gentleman with a ruddy complexion and graying temples who introduced himself and asked him to sit down. Wallmoden did not understand his name.

For some reason Wallmoden imagined he was sitting across from a Hungarian.

"The Baroness Pistohlkors," said the stranger, "telephoned me to say that you would be so kind as to bring me" – and he pointed to the table on which it still lay unopened – "this letter.

I thank you very much. A charming lady, this Baroness! Isn't that so?"

"Yes," replied Wallmoden," charming... but also so beautiful that you must certainly regret not having received her letter personally."

The stranger offered him a cigarette.

"I meet the Baroness now and again. Early on I used to see her more often. She is, by the way, the woman with probably the best legs I have ever seen."

"Strange you should mention it," said Wallmoden.

"Why strange?"

"Because you continue the thoughts I just had."

"I don't find that so strange."

"No?"

"No."

"Why not?"

"Because you no doubt observed her as she left you. Even so, she is a very attractive person. Certainly, as she departed, you could observe her without interruption. Then her legs must have caught your attention."

He lit Wallmoden's cigarette.

Wallmoden stared at him.

"Are you surprised by this?" asked the stranger. "It is simply logical. By the way, since we are speaking about such things, I don't share the momentary fascination with attractive legs. I consider it even a bit shallow to appreciate something that cannot express a sense of understanding or spirit. Personally, I would rather look at beautiful eyes. Although I must admit that good legs remain a contemporary interest. Certainly, women did not have such beautiful legs in the past."

"You think so?" asked Wallmoden.

"I am even convinced of it. The legs of a woman that have impressed me the most are not even particularly beautiful."

"That's sad," commented Wallmoden.

"Not entirely." Suddenly, and without any seeming connection, the stranger asked, "Have you been to Rome? You probably missed the most interesting sights."

"How so?"

"Or at least *the* most interesting sight. Do you know the Thermea Museum? In the courtyard, which is said to have been designed by Michelangelo, there are many boring Roman statues of depressingly gray stone, which were obviously sufficient to enchant the Roman journeyers of the eighteenth century. But there is, I believe, if one goes into the west wing, a cabinet, illuminated by a glass ceiling. The observer cannot help but become breathless at the sight of the only, and incredibly beautiful, figure in the room: a young girl or woman posing with a dolphin – an Aphrodite of Paros marble, which casts off a shine of a wax or honey color, causing the figure to appear as if it were surrounded by incense or a fog of gold. Its head and arms are missing, but one assumes from the pose of the upper torso that she has emerged from the sea and is wringing the water from her hair. There is reason to believe that she is none other than the famous Anadyomene, which Apelles modeled after an acquaintance of Alexander the Great, in such a wonderful fashion that the king ultimately gave the maiden to the artist."

"Charming," said Wallmoden. "After all, the women of the entire world were available to the conquerors. Perhaps this was the most benevolent use of her he could have made with his power. And I absolutely agree that the most beautiful should find its way to the best. Usually it finds its way to the worst. My God, how happy the sculptor and how unhappy the maiden must have been! By the way, what is this praiseworthy piece called?"

"The Aphrodite of Kyrene," answered the stranger, as he removed the lid of a jar of bonbons that stood on the table, and offered them to Wallmoden. "Nevertheless," he continued, "the legs of this godly creation, which I fell in love with at first sight, are not the best. And, for example, the legs of Helena or the red-haired Phryne, or the white Prokris may also leave something to be desired. This is simply the style of the period. Even Alcibiades or Antinous are hard to imagine in riding boots. They would have appeared too heavy. We ourselves are reduced by exactly the same measure of the strength of the clothing layers that cover us. By the way, where did you get the boots you are wearing? They are a fine pair."

"Oh," said Wallmoden and looked down at them, "I already had these in the war. They are over twenty years old and they are the only pair I have left."

"The only pair? Then I would advise you to have a second pair made. And soon."

"Why?"

"Because you will need them."

"You mean..."

"Absolutely. Otherwise you will not have the opportunity again to order another pair."

"Otherwise?"

"To be sure. I am taking the liberty to wonder why you are still even here."

"I too, wonder why," answered Wallmoden after a pause as he looked at his watch. "Perhaps because you have been so entertaining! Well I hope you will now excuse me." He stood up.

"What? You want to leave already?" said the stranger.

"I have an appointment."

"With the Baroness again, no doubt?"

"Why do you think that?"

"I don't only think that, I know it."

"Did she find it necessary to tell you about that as well?" asked Wallmoden.

"No," laughed the stranger. "Naturally, she didn't say one

word about it."

"Then how else can you determine this?"

"When one knows," answered the stranger, "that one will be going out with a lady, one doesn't wear boots, even your fine pair. One also wears trousers. Therefore, your appointment must have been made very recently. You have had no opportunity to change. And you have not been in the company of any lady aside from the Baroness. It therefore follows that you are going out with the Baroness."

"You are right yet again," sighed Wallmoden. "So you are probably also aware that I must go now."

"Oh do stay a bit longer!" said the stranger. "It has been so amusing and I am bored when I am alone. But I am not ashamed of it. There is nothing more wretched then people who insist they are never bored."

"Nevertheless, I am sorry, I must go."

"Women tend to be late."

"But not always."

"Stay anyway. If a woman arrives on time, and the man who should be waiting for her is not there, she will leave – even if she cares for him – only to return later and pretend as if she were also late. If she doesn't care for him, well then, the rendezvous wasn't meant to be."

"That too may be right," said Wallmoden. "It may be a platitude, but it is correct, as sadly all platitudes are."

"Right," answered the stranger. "And mostly that which is wrong comes from individual consciousness. It is as if humanity wanted to express an aversion to reality, one that is completely lacking in fantasy."

"You think so?"

"Yes. Even the worst writer is able to create better stories than life itself. It is only tolerable for us because we lead our lives in a totally unrealistic fashion. There is nothing more hopeless than to be caught between the millstones of life. A person becomes just like everyone else."

"I don't completely agree with you," commented Wallmoden. "I have had the feeling, particularly recently, that life could also be very full of fantasy."

"That speaks only for you," said the stranger. "If you look closely, you will find that you have done everything to make it so, while life has done nothing."

Wallmoden, who was interested in the direction of this conversation, was about to reply, when the stranger stood up and said he did not wish to delay him any longer. It might be possible that Baroness Pistohlkors might really be waiting. And with that, he escorted his guest into the foyer and bid him farewell – almost as abruptly as he had bid him welcome.

As Wallmoden sat in his car, he began to think about the conversation. Even if it was only intended to pass a quarter-hour with polite phrases, it was conducted with such skillfulness by the stranger that Wallmoden never found the opportunity to observe the room in which it took place, nor to study the actual traits of his conversation partner. The room had dissolved around the constant talk. A small incident had occurred as Wallmoden had left the apartment. A person approached him in the dark hallway that lead to the quarters of the caretaker, but turned around immediately when Wallmoden became visible. Wallmoden attributed this quick retreat to his uniform, and above all, his neck decoration. It was, incidentally, a very insignificant order. He was awarded it as an orderly officer during a brief stint in Constantinople.

It was definitely quite some time after eight when he stopped in front of Pistohlkors's building, but she was not waiting. He lit a cigarette and glanced up at the row of windows. The building was old-fashioned and unattractive. It occurred to him that both

Pistohlkors and the stranger lived in similar circumstances. The stranger's house was even uglier.

Pistohlkors appeared after a few minutes. She wore a hint of jewelry and a white coat over her dress, an evening coat with a pleated and ruffled collar.

"Who was the man you sent me to see?" asked Wallmoden.

"Didn't you like him?" she inquired.

"Yes, very much. But who was he?"

"A certain Herr von Oertel." She was silent for a moment and then asked, "Where are we going?"

"Wherever you wish."

He thought she would suggest the Kahlenberg or the Prater amusement park. Instead she asked: "To the Grand Hotel?"

"Fine," he replied. They got into the car and she sat close to him. Her silks rustled gently in the dark and her jewelry glittered on her like dew.

They drove up the Salesianergasse and across the Rennweg.

He greeted a few officers as they entered the lobby of the Grand Hotel. She wanted to know who they were.

"I don't know them," he said. "But why don't you tell me who you are?"

"But you know that already."

"Actually, I don't even know your first name."

"Well, I don't either."

"What does that mean?"

"I would have to check my passport first."

"Whatever for?"

"I am an adventuress," she laughed. "And I have forgotten the first name in my passport. I would really have to look."

"Seriously," he said, "what is your name?"

"Seriously," she replied, "it makes no difference if I am named Marie or Irene or Rose of Lima. I am called Cuba, like the island. But it is pronounced 'Kyooba.'"

"How did you get a name like that?"

"I was called Kouba as a girl. It is a Czech name. My parents emigrated when I was still a child. I went to school in Sioux Falls, a small city in the American Midwest." She pronounced it like *Souh-Falls*. "Since then," she explained, "people have used my surname as my only name."

He looked at her. "And the man," he asked, "whom you married? The Pistohlkors are, as best I know, Balts."

"My husband is dead," she replied. "But he wasn't a Balt. He had a German passport. By the way, he was my second husband."

"And your first?"

"He divorced me. I could also say that I divorced him, but it was really he who divorced me."

By now the waiters were waiting.

"Well, fine then," said Wallmoden and started to order. She wanted to eat lightly and ordered the scampi with strawberries to follow. It was rather warm in the restaurant, so they let their coats fall over the backs of their chairs. Her dress was sleeveless, and for a moment, as she allowed her coat to fall, the tips of her breasts impressed themselves into the thin cloth of her dress.

A few people observed them with interest, particularly an elderly gentleman, a Herr von Nebentisch, who had a meaty, perhaps a bit of an apoplectic coloring, and who watched them from beneath bushy eyebrows and with tilted head. The whites of his eyes were the color of old ivory. With awkward fingers, which now and again pushed up his cuffs, he cracked nuts. Wallmoden gave him a noticeable glance, and the man returned to gazing at his plate.

"And how long have you been back?" asked Wallmoden after some time.

"Back where?" she asked.

"In Europe."

"For three years. It was my husband's idea, since neither of us had any success at the film studio where we met."

"Whom did you meet there? Your first or second husband?"

"My second. My first husband was an employee in Sioux Falls. My father was then still working as a tailor. Later he got the notion of publishing a religious magazine, which finally destroyed him. The Midwest is so boring that people get the most unbelievable ideas. One day my husband appeared at my father's shop and ordered a suit. He first saw me there and stayed on because of me. I was only seventeen and the marriage didn't last very long. Sometime after our wedding we decided to buy some household things. There was something on which we could not agree, I think it was the purchase of a brush. We argued and then my husband angrily walked out of the store and left me there.

"A few minutes earlier someone had stolen a few things from the store. As my husband tried to leave – naturally without paying, since we hadn't decided on anything – he was held as the thief, or at least the accomplice. Since he hardly defended himself, he was arrested. His anger at me robbed him of all thought. He never forgave me and later divorced me."

"Yes, well," said Wallmoden after a moment, "decisions of importance are often only brought about by misunderstandings – or even through the result of absentmindedness."

"It was really not a decision of any importance."

"One only acts reasonably in situations of unimportance."

"It wasn't unreasonable."

He shrugged. "I don't know," he said, "I haven't been married to you yet. And your second husband?"

"My second husband was an actor. But he only got small parts. He was very tall. He had consumption. At any rate, he was difficult to film because of his height, so when he shot a love scene, his partner always had to stand on a pedestal. Pinchot might have been a good match for him, but she poisoned herself."

"It is strange how many actresses poison themselves," replied

Wallmoden.

"It is even stranger that they first go to the trouble to become actresses. Well, it was on the beach at Santa Monica that we decided to get married, my second husband and I, and it happened like this: I was infatuated with one of the lifeguards back then. At every beach there is a boat which is manned by those who save the bathing guests who find themselves drowning in the surf. They are also swimming instructors, but above all, they must stay at the beach all day, so that one has something to look at.

"I never cared much for gaunt men, and as I sat there with one of these lifeguards, Pistohlkors, whom I knew from the studio, approached us in his bathing suit. We both laughed, but Pistohlkors, who was not very quick, or at least pretended not to notice, joined us and began to court me. This upset the lifeguard, and since I had laughed at Pistohlkors, he felt justified in asking him to leave. There was an exchange of words and finally he insulted Pistohlkors. Without a moment's hesitation, Pistohlkors grabbed him. It was as if the farm boy had attacked a buffalo. In the space of a minute, he had hit the ground three times. On the third fall, he remained there. He was helped up and I married him a few days later. Unfortunately, he received an inheritance soon thereafter, and we were able to return to Europe. The Californian climate had been beneficial, but the European one didn't agree with him, and he died in a few months."

"And you still believe that you really cared for him?" asked Wallmoden.

"Yes," she insisted. "Sometimes our heart is even stronger than our bad taste. For example, I know a woman who is married to a foreign officer and loves him dearly, even though he is supposedly the most battle-injured man of his country."

"Even Nelson," said Wallmoden," despite his one eye and one arm, was loved by Lady Hamilton – by the most beautiful woman of her time."

"If you truly love someone," she replied, " and you are missing both eyes, you can still see them; and if both arms are missing, you can still embrace them."

He was silent. "And from where do you know this Herr von Oertel?" he asked sometime later.

She did not answer him right away. "From a group of people," she said finally, "whose letter you gave him."

"And who are these people?" he asked.

She gave no reply but instead stared at her plate with knitted brows. He looked at her and after a few moments apologized for having bored her. She remained silent. When the waiter brought her scampi, she picked at them absentmindedly, and around nine-thirty she asked Wallmoden to take her home.

"Home, really?" he asked.

"Yes, really."

When he stopped in front of her building in the Salesianergasse, she remained seated in the car. He said something, but she did not answer, and he took it to be an invitation. He kissed her cheek and she allowed it to happen without moving; but it seemed to him as if he had heard her sigh. Only when he became a bit more passionate did she finally offer resistance.

"May I see you again?" he asked.

They agreed that he should come by on an evening of another day.

As she walked into the building, he was convinced that she had acted this way in order to be able to go out again. He drove a bit into the Strohgasse, returned by foot, and observed the building's entrance. He waited – with a sense of satisfaction, as he admitted to himself – in vain.

Around ten-thirty he drove home.

The sky above his car was set with such an unusual amount

of stars, that they appeared to be like the gold dust that the conquistadors sent overseas to their kings. Gold dust from leather sacks, spilled onto black Spanish velvet.

3

The next morning, Wallmoden's squadron drove – the regiment was motorized – battle-ready to the town of Wuermla about twenty kilometers distant, left the vehicles at the edge of the town, and exercised an attack on a pretend enemy. Wallmoden led the drill because the squadron leader, Herr von Kaufmann, had been ordered to attend a conference. Since the marksmen troops had come across the crests of the hills, which surrounded the village, he had a peculiar experience. It was completely an internal one, and he rightly believed that no one else had noticed it. He had curiously desired to forget it as soon as possible. Why he wanted to forget it, he couldn't say – perhaps he had the feeling of having been pulled into something very negative.

The hill over which he and the squadron troops followed the first two squads, was covered with oats, which, although they had begun to ripen, had not yet been harvested. On one side of the hill lay the town. Slowly marching along the yellow path of grain, Wallmoden considered a thought that had occupied him for a few minutes at least since the first attack wave had disappeared over the hill and from his view.

He considered that there had been no harvest, and what he meant was the *entire* harvest. Nothing – he heard himself say – nothing occurs before its time, and nothing will be harvested until it is ripe. Suddenly he had an unusually exact, almost overwhelming sense of time. Time, he said to himself, is a following of things. Just as two things cannot occupy the same space, there is also the same temporal condition. The place where one body finds itself cannot be the same for another body – if the first body is still there. Time is as impenetrable as matter. Certainly time is invisible, said Wallmoden to himself, and that is why people are so inexact about it. In reality, it is as exact as space. And he sensed the exactness of time. The world seemed like a giant clockwork to him, an astrolabe, a monstrously large astronomical device, on which not only the stars, but all things move and shine in temporal and spatial exactitude. A person may err, but not a thing. Therefore it would be laughable to have believed that the stalks that moved in the oat field, and the dust clouds caused by the stepping on the field path, did not move themselves with the same exactness as the stars. But the dust moved *now*, and the stalks moved *now*, and a time must come which would be different from the present (since two times cannot occupy one time, one space) and the stalks would be ripe then and they would be reaped. The corn and the wheat were already there, also the poppies had sleepily deflowered themselves, but the oats still stood. They were not yet ripe. Only when it is cut is the harvest in. The harvest is the mane of the earth. It was not time yet.

During these thoughts, which he was happy to end – he had suddenly lost the thread – he had passed over the hill and now he saw the town. After a few more steps, he found himself (it had already started on the previous slope) in a kind of flat depression, which was pushed into the back of the hill like a weak fingerprint in dough. This depression had no buildings, but was covered with grass (as if cattle grazed here) between the fields, and singular rocks peeked up from that grass.

The sun was stinging with extraordinary strength at this moment, and it was possible that the circular form of the depression increased the light-headedness Wallmoden felt from the heat. At any rate, he felt himself becoming dizzy as he stepped into the depression. He had the feeling he had entered into the center of a weak whirlwind. He also imagined that the ground smelled of thyme. From this moment on, his feeling of dizziness became very strong. It seemed to him that not only light and wind, but also another shimmering substance whirled around him.

He felt as if he were surrounded by a circle of people, more -perhaps two or three circles – which moved alternatingly in opposite directions; the circles were made up of pairs which danced and sang. They did not turn around each other, but they pushed each other along, faces close together, sideways. The female dancers stood on the feet of the male dancers, who lifted them with each step. The pairs made four sideways steps following the direction of the circle, after which they again made three side steps in the opposite direction, so that they only moved one place in seven steps. The figures shone. It seemed to Wallmoden (and he truly felt that this could be nothing more than a fantasy caused by illness) that they shone in the same manner in which things seem to shine to someone who is falling unconscious or who has nicotine poisoning. Suddenly he noticed that the figures were naked. Their skin shone in the burning sun as if dripping with oil. He believed the dancers had not been naked before, but had disrobed. It was a sacred nakedness.

At this moment, the opposing movements of the circles united themselves into a single unit, like a watch spring, and they banded ever tighter around Wallmoden, as if they were elastic, in a spiral, so that the song of the dancers in this close proximity was like a howling in his ears. He felt their breath like a wild snarl and their odor was so strong that Wallmoden nearly lost consciousness. The dance was gone now. It was pure obscenity, as suddenly a shadow fell from above, and the vision, or whatever it was, extinguished itself in a spiral and disappeared.

The edge of a cloud pulled across the sun. He suddenly noticed that the men of the squadron were helping him up from his knees. They thought he might have stumbled on a rock in the grass. Ahead of the third wave, Lieutenant Rex made his way over the hill toward him. Wallmoden mumbled something unintelligible – the Lieutenant should assemble the squadron.

He recovered quickly and just a few minutes later he believed his experience had never happened. The sun remained hidden. Storm clouds grew in the sky and emptied themselves during the return trip. The rain fell in a glittering rush and the thunder, especially when lightning struck nearby, sounded like shots from silver guns.

That afternoon there was a guest: Herr von Baumgarten, who owned the nearby estate of Schoenbuehl. He entertained the officers of the regiment and also took part in the entertainment of the casino.

The meal had already started when Sodoma entered. In an expected manner, he assured Wallmoden that he was appearing "in the flesh" and "not yet" as a spirit.

Wallmoden thanked him earnestly for this conveyance and added that the Cavalry Captain probably has no idea how important such assurances can sometimes be.

"Why important?" asked Sodoma.

Wallmoden had been prepared to remark on his late morning's experience, but suddenly felt a resistance to mentioning anything about it. Instead Wallmoden replied that at the very least he hoped the Cavalry Captain would be honest when reporting his condition.

What reason would Wallmoden have to believe that he would not tell the truth, asked Sodoma.

Perhaps due to the spirit's sense of shame, explained Wallmoden. But the untruth would not help the Cavalry Captain very much. A spirit would be easy to differentiate from a living person.

"Naturally. It is transparent," said Sodoma, who had satisfied himself that Wallmoden was playing along with his ghostly comedy.

"Or it might wear a white sheet."

"I didn't mean that," said Wallmoden. "It would appear in its essence."

"What does that mean?" asked Sodoma, and even Lieutenant Obentraut, who had begun to listen with interest, inquired as to what exactly Wallmoden meant by the essence of a spirit.

"The spirit," said Wallmoden, "is the essence of the body. A ghost would appear more or less as the living being had."

"Therefore," remarked Obentraut, "the spirits would have to be naked."

Wallmoden was dumbfounded. "How do you know that?" he asked. Sodoma called out, "Have you ever seen a naked spirit?"

"No," replied Obentraut. "I have never seen a spirit."

"That's a pity," said Sodoma, "especially for someone like you, who always talks about it. And why do you believe that a spirit must be undressed?"

"Because clothes don't belong to the body," replied Obentraut. "And therefore, as Wallmoden said, since the spirit represents the body, it doesn't represent the clothing with it, and so the spirit is naked."

"I didn't mean that," explained Wallmoden. "Rather, I am of the opinion that a spirit must represent the essence of the physical. Clothing can also be part of that, since it is often very characteristic of the individuality of the person."

"Exactly," said Sodoma. "But even if it didn't follow in that way, I would still resist being a nudist. Even more so, I promise to appear in a uniform, or at least in civilian garb."

"Why then are there so many reports about spirits appearing

in bed sheets?" asked Obentraut.

"Perhaps," answered Wallmoden, "this might be so because death, or the way of death, was characteristic for those in question. Most people's lives run along without significance. The only interesting thing in their lives is ultimately death."

"I think you are overestimating death," said Sodoma. "It is hardly an extraordinary achievement. Anyone can die, must die, because everything dies. It can't be more interesting than life."

"On the contrary," said Baumgarten, "it is, after all, the only experience which, for example, forces a being who lived without spirit an entire lifetime, to give up the spirit."

"Well," said Sodoma, "there might have been people who have died without spirit."

"In theory," said Obentraut, "it must be possible for animals also to have spirits."

"I don't know," said Wallmoden. "I don't know if spiriting is even possible. It might well be pure imagination to believe one has actually seen a ghost."

"You said it yourself, that your great-grandfather had passed through the camp of Santa Lucia while he was actually sleeping. Do you think that his spirit sat on his horse, or the spirit of his horse?"

"I can't exactly tell you," replied Wallmoden. "I have honestly never thought about it."

"Does anyone know where the horse was at the time?"

Major Dombaste, who had this time followed this entire discussion in silence, wrinkled his forehead and threw a disapproving glance at Obentraut.

"No one knows," said Wallmoden. "But I don't think it's that important. It is only important to know if our entire life is spiritual or if it is only what is generally known as real. In other words, are we in fact humans or only a form of spirit?"

"Yes," said Dombaste, "and this very consideration appears

very problematic to me. Actually, I would advise the gentlemen, and particularly you, dear Obentraut, to approach more controllable themes, especially since the inspiration of all these discussions – the drowned maiden, whose corpse was of such great interest to our friend Mauritz – has turned up in the meantime."

Mauritz bowed his head as the Major spoke his name.

"Really?" asked First Lieutenant Hertzberg. "It's been found? Where was it?"

"In the river," answered Mauritz tersely.

"Why didn't you tell us?"

"My God," said Mauritz, "it just appeared."

"When was it found?"

"Yesterday afternoon," said Mauritz.

"Regarding yesterday afternoon," and Sodoma again turned to Wallmoden, "I very much regret that you had to meet that boring person at our place, this Pistohlkors, or whatever her name is."

"She wasn't all that boring," said Wallmoden.

"No?"

"No. I took her home and she was rather entertaining during the trip."

"Well," said Sodoma, "the cat hardly had her tongue, but she did have a mania about only speaking to my wife. Even my wife thought it strange and told me she doesn't understand it."

"Oh well," sighed Wallmoden, "later, probably because no one else was around, she even spoke to me."

"Weren't you also on the Piaristengasse yesterday?" asked Kaufmann, Wallmoden's squadron chief.

"On the Piaristengasse? Yes," said Wallmoden and was puzzled that Kaufmann would know this.

Kaufmann felt the need to explain: "I believe I saw your car parked there."

"Were you also in Vienna?" asked Wallmoden.

"Naturally."

Wallmoden raised his brows. When he had requested leave from Kaufmann and asked him if he would like to join him, Kaufmann had thanked him and clearly expressed the desire to stay where he was.

"That is to say," Kaufmann added as he obviously recalled the same moment, "I decided to go later. Too bad I didn't ride with you. We could have dined together. Really too bad." He appreciated a good meal.

At about two o'clock, they rose and prepared to leave. As they moved to leave the casino, Baumgarten approached Wallmoden and requested he stay and chat a while.

Wallmoden was somewhat surprised, but he said that it would be a pleasure.

Herr von Baumgarten had the reputation of being a unique person, something he was not in the least. Perhaps he simply made fewer mistakes than some. He credited his cleverness to an attentive observation of people, who, as he claimed, continued to interest him far more than the cows or books that would usually fill out the life of a landowner. He had formed his own history and philosophy based on the occurrences in the area and above all, on the society of the city. Apparently he knew about everything, including everyone's personal details, but he was liked because, although he had heard much, he rarely found it worth the trouble to pass it along.

He stared intently at Wallmoden for a few minutes before he started to speak.

"Count Wallmoden," he finally said, "I hope you will not misunderstand what I am about to say. You have not served for about twenty years, and you have only served again for about two days. Perhaps you have forgotten a few things in the meantime, perhaps a few things have changed since then. You were a standard bearer in the war, yes? I have never been a soldier, and that is why I find it difficult to tell you what I would like to say, but tell you I must. Particularly, I would like to suggest you never forget what you represent in society and in public life."

"Certainly not," replied an amazed Wallmoden. "And I believe I have never forgotten it. Nevertheless," he paused a moment to think, "I did make the faux pas of going out with a lady while wearing my riding boots. But I had no opportunity to change. Was this a matter for discussion here? Perhaps it would have been wiser to have driven to Vienna in my civilian clothes. This possibility had slipped my mind since it had previously been forbidden – at least for us."

Baumgarten didn't seem to fully comprehend what he meant. "I wanted to advise you," he continued, "to be a bit more discriminating with your choice of surroundings. It is possible that you know people from some time ago, whose company I would no longer recommend – and it might have been better if you hadn't gotten to know such people in the first place. The society one found oneself in after the war was hardly distinguished. Take the opportunity to abandon it now."

After a moment Wallmoden replied: "Herr von Baumgarten, I believe it certainly does not represent the current view to reproach me for having gone out with a lady simply because she is the daughter of common people."

Baumgarten blinked. "Who is the daughter of common people?" he asked.

"The lady who went out with me."

"Really?" said Baumgarten, and it seemed he did not know how to reply to this. "I had no idea. May I inquire what this lady's name is?"

"Pistohlkors. Baroness Pistohlkors. That her father was a

tailor should not be astonishing."

"You think so? I mean, I wanted to say, you believe so?"

"Absolutely. As a child she emigrated to America with her parents, was raised there, married an American first, whose name she did not tell me, and then a Baron von Pistohlkors – which should be sufficient to make her acceptable to society. In between her marriages she had been active in the film industry..."

"In film?"

"Yes, and I don't consider this to be any sort of blemish. You must understand that there is nothing curious about her career. On the contrary, she is an absolutely attractive, well-dressed person with excellent manners."

Baumgarten stared at him. "Tell me," he said, after a few seconds, "isn't she the same person you discussed earlier with Cavalry Captain von Sodoma?"

"Certainly. I first met her in his, or rather his in-laws' apartment."

"In Sodoma's apartment?"

"Yes."

"So, not on the Piaristengasse?"

"No. She asked me to deliver a letter there."

"A..."

"Yes, a letter."

"On the Piaristengasse?"

"Of course. May I ask if you have any complaint against this lady?'

Baumgarten hesitated. "What made you take a letter there?"

"I offered to take it."

"You did?"

"I did. She said that she needed to do so, but I suggested she could change while I delivered it."

"And what did the letter say?"

"I really don't know. It is even possible she didn't know."

"Why would she not have known?"

"Because she hadn't written it. She had been asked by friends to deliver it. At least that is what she claimed."

"What sort of friends?"

"She didn't tell me."

"When did you first make her acquaintance?" asked Baumgarten.

"Yesterday."

"Only yesterday?"

"Yes. I already told you. During my visit to Frau von Sodoma."

"And Frau von Sodoma? Had she known this... this lady for some time already?"

"No, I don't think so. She had supposedly only met her a few days before."

"Where was this?"

"At a social gathering."

"Which one?"

"At some gathering I know nothing about. May I know why Cavalry Captain von Sodoma is reproaching me for the company of a woman who was sitting in his own apartment?"

"The Cavalry Captain?"

"Yes. Anyway, he couldn't stand her from the very start."

"The Cavalry Captain has nothing to do with her."

"Well then, who else has seen me with her?"

Baumgarten did not answer right away. He stood up, walked to the window and looked outside. Then he came back and sat in his chair. "Perhaps," he finally said, "this whole thing is nothing more than a case of mistaken identity."

"Obviously. I would hope so. Mistaken with whom?"

"Excuse me?"

"I mean, whom has the Baroness been mistaken for?"

Baumgarten shrugged. "I don't know. But try to describe her."

"As you know, it is difficult to describe a woman," said Wallmoden. "It's actually completely impossible."

"You think so?"

"Yes. Many women have been described as beautiful, but we still cannot imagine what they looked like. For example, don't you also believe that Homer had truly attempted to describe Helena? But ultimately all we know – and not from him, but from others – is that she was the most beautiful woman in the world. What does this really mean? Nothing. In reality, she might indeed have been so beautiful that one would be breathless at the sight of her, as it happened to the elders as she passed the Scythian Gate. Homer is at least able to describe the reaction. But we know nothing about her as a person. We don't know her height, nor what kind of eyes or hair she had. What we do know is that she did not have particularly attractive legs."

Baumgarten had started to drum on the table with his fingers and might have been ready to say that the subject is not the beauty of Helena, but the visage of Baroness Pistohlkors. He stopped drumming after Wallmoden had discounted Helena's legs. "How would you know that?" he asked.

"Herr von Oertel mentioned it," said Wallmoden.

"Herr von Oertel?" bellowed Baumgarten.

"Yes. The man to whom I delivered Pistohlkors's letter."

"He said that?"

"Yes. Why not?"

"He spoke with you about Helena?"

"And not only about her, as far as I can remember, but also about Phryne, Procris and Alcibiades. He told me they all had unattractive legs."

"Really?" said the puzzled Baumgarten. "And how does he know this?"

"It is a theory of his."

"And you didn't talk about anything else."

"Hardly."

"Why so?"

"Because the inspiration of the entire discussion had been the legs of Baroness Pistohlkors – which are really rather nice. Yes, he even said they may be the most attractive legs he has ever seen."

"Well then," said Baumgarten, "at least we have the beginnings of a description. Pistohlkors has nice legs."

"Outstanding ones, actually."

"But what else did you discuss?"

"My boots."

"Your..."

"Yes."

"...and?"

"And then he told me I should have a second pair made."

"You can certainly do that. But what else did you talk about?"

"I told him I had an appointment."

"With the lady?"

"Yes. I didn't mention that. But he..."

"Doesn't he know her personally?"

"Who?"

"This Baroness."

"Yes. He said he sees her now and again."

Baumgarten held a steady gaze on him. "What sort of a reputation does she actually have, this woman?"

"I have no idea," answered Wallmoden. "It seems she was a bit odd with Frau von Sodoma."

"How so?"

"She spoke only with her and ignored the Cavalry Captain and me as if we didn't exist."

"But now she no longer acts as if you do not exist?"

"No. She is actually very amusing."

After a moment, Baumgarten appeared as if he would ask yet

another question, but he stood up instead. Wallmoden stood as well. Baumgarten reached for a box of cigarettes lying on the table and offered it to him. "Are you in some way interested in this woman?" he asked.

"I haven't had the opportunity to think about it," said Wallmoden as he took a cigarette.

"You have it now – this opportunity."

"Really?"

"Absolutely."

"If I may be frank," Wallmoden said, "I still do not know what it is you want, Herr von Baumgarten. What is your interest in this woman? What do you really know about her?"

"Let us suppose," said Baumgarten as he gazed out the window, "that she does not have a good reputation."

"But that is no reason..."

"It is no longer as it was," said Baumgarten. "I have already told you that. Are you interested in her or not? You have only spent a single evening in her company. It isn't possible that you could already be so taken by her."

"My God," said Wallmoden, "up to now I have found her to be an attractive person."

"Yes, indeed", said Baumgarten. "But about how many others has that also been said!"

And they left the casino.

4

As Wallmoden thought about the conversation, he tried to determine whether Cuba's bad reputation actually bothered him or not. In truth, her reputation was not *that* bad. One could perhaps not use her to represent a good reputation – that was all.

What does a reputation actually mean? There are women who have a great many affairs and keep them secret so they appear respectable. There are others who are the friend of one man for an entire lifetime and have the most questionable of reputations. And women who don't risk a bad reputation, at least for a time, are not women. There are those who are truly capable of loving and others that can never love, and that is the entire difference – or at least ought to be the entire difference. The concept of a reputation, Wallmoden thought, is a complete misunderstanding. It only describes the manner in which we *see* things. But how do we see things? Usually, completely in error. One should see things as they really *are*. But who can do this? And perhaps it would not be so good to do this after all. We live off our illusions, Oertel had said. If one did not have the illusion, even with a respectable woman, that she is capable of anything – or at least many things – there would be nothing more desolate than a respectable woman. She need not have to translate her possibilities into actions, but she has to have them. The possibility of having them is absolutely everything.

As he dwelt on these thoughts, Wallmoden encountered

Senior-Officer-Cadet Rosthorn, who had been with the regiment for some time now. Wallmoden asked him if it would be possible to leave the camp without being seen following afternoon duty – sometime between four and seven – and if this would also be possible, for example, after eleven o'clock in the evening.

"Where do you want to go?" asked Rosthorn.

"To Vienna."

"The Chief is giving a dinner tonight. Major Dombaste and Cavalry Captain Sodoma have also been requested to attend."

"Fine," said Wallmoden. "I would like to leave before or after the dinner. I have an errand in Vienna."

"To leave after dinner will be difficult" advised Rosthorn. "This celebration might take some time, and you cannot excuse yourself without good reason. On the other hand, I assume your arriving in Vienna around four a.m. wouldn't do you any good. Or am I wrong?"

"No," said Wallmoden. "I will need to leave right after duty."

"In civilian clothes?"

"Yes, of course."

"Then you must pass through the Porta Decumana."

Rostohorn, who was classically educated in a most thorough manner, liked to compare the camp to a Roman legion. And there were similarities. "Don't you notice," Rosthorn mused, "that everything from the eagles to the belt buckle is like that of the Romans? And even given certain deviations," he added with a barely noticeable smile, "the essence, the style, is still the same. The entire organization of this war machine has only one counterpart – the Romans." He referred to the main gate as the Porta Praetoria and the one in the rear, leading to the parade ground, as the Decumana. To his disappointment however, the direction of the Via Principalis did not connect with the main road of the camp, and he was also unhappy with the other deviations from Roman order. The effect of this – as he insisted

– would be felt in time.

"I can't drive through the Decumana with my car," said Wallmoden. "I mean, I could get through, but then I would not be able to escape through the parade ground."

He looked between the motor pool garages to the parade ground where the squadrons were drilling. The sun shone on the long row of helmets and the voice of Lieutenant Rex echoed loudly. The sky, cleansed by the storm, was stretched out like a tent of blue silk.

These afternoon drills were Wallmoden's favorite because they reminded him of a time when, also during the afternoon, he attempted to teach his cavalry the grips of a carbine and a respectable march tempo. "Afternoon business" is what they called it then. But there had also been a kind of tradition at the time, which made a saber far handier than a gun, and above all, if one didn't ride, one moved about clumsier than a fish on land.

All these many differences had passed on, along with the red trousers and the horsemanship. If one looked at the parade ground now, there was only the undistinguished gray of today.

"Then try to disappear through the Porta Praetoria," suggested Rosthorn.

But it appeared as if this would not be possible. Immediately following the drill, Kaufmann requested a drive up the Danube. He conversed with him during the entire trip and asked him in a detailed and a concerned manner about his interests and living conditions. Wallmoden, who first wondered about this, finally accepted the possibility that Kaufmann cared enough about his officers to dedicate an entire afternoon to such discussions...

The dinner, which took place at the best inn of the town, left nothing to be desired. As Rosthorn had correctly guessed, it lasted until almost three. Wallmoden found an opportunity to talk about Pistohlkors with Sodoma.

"As enticing as the Baroness is," he felt duty-bound to explain, "as enticing as she is – or perhaps because she is so enticing – she seems to be better company for gentlemen than for your wife."

"Really?" Sodoma replied immediately. "You know that already? At our place, at any rate, she seemed to prefer the company of women."

He declined any further discussion along this line.

Kaufmann had planned the meal with great success and there was a considerable amount of drinking. At the end, Rosthorn gave a speech, which was laced with Latin quotes and was so long that it became an event displacing the meal. It began to become dawn as they drove back. Yet the red star, which Wallmoden noticed in the Strohgasse, still hung singularly in the sky. It had started to move westward. A second star with a cold glare, like an eye of glass, approached the zenith.

Pistohlkors lived in rented rooms in the first floor of the building in the Salesianergasse. Wallmoden had already visited the entrance to that building with some frequency. Outside the windows of her apartment there was a small yard which was connected to the rear garden. The evening sun shone through the branches of the trees and played across the figure of a young woman who sat up from a divan as Wallmoden entered. It was as if she had emerged from water, the waves still playing around her and the clothes she was wearing: satin trousers and a morning coat of silk, shimmering as if she had just stepped from the tides. She sat at the edge of the divan as her feet searched for her slippers.

"I must apologize for not having come yesterday," said Wallmoden. "It was simply impossible, rather, it was made impossible for me. I wanted to ring you, but I could not find your name in the telephone book. And also information had failed to find it."

"Well," she said with a trace of a smile on her lips, "that is why you are here today."

"Naturally."

She took him in with one glance. He was dressed in civilian clothes.

"And I consider it especially dear of you," he added, "that you didn't allow your presence to be denied." (He meant: because she wasn't dressed.)

"Oh, this," she said after a pause. "I am not going out until later."

"With me, I hope."

"Unfortunately not. I have an appointment. I had no idea that you would actually come."

"Couldn't you have assumed it?"

"I thought you were probably no longer here."

"It is really amazing," he said, "how the entire world seems to believe I am long gone."

"Those sort of people always stay the longest," she replied and offered him a cigarette. She stood quite close and he noticed her scent. Although tall, she was a bit shorter than him, and she reached his eyes. Her face, particularly the line of her cheeks, still showed an unbelievable youthfulness. A hair-clip with tiny diamonds sparkled in her hair. Standing, she moved her body in an almost imperceptible fashion. On the high heels of her shoes, it was as if, with a forward leaning motion and with downcast eyes, she were offering him the rosebuds of her breasts.

Although this woman did not have a fine reputation, he managed not to stare. He looked away, took a cigarette and sat down on the divan.

"Well?" she asked after a moment. "What have you done in the meantime?"

"I raved about you," he said.

"For what reason?" she wanted to know.

"You are reason enough," he replied. "But I also told others about you."

"Really? Whom for example?"

"A certain Herr von Baumgarten," he said. "Do you know him? No? Well, he acted as if he knew about you. It seems someone has told him we were out together."

"Herr von Sodoma?"

"He had no idea. It had to have been someone else."

"And that person passed it on?"

"Yes," he said. "Strange, isn't it? Or perhaps even more so, it isn't strange! It is completely understandable that one is noticed when one appears with such a bewitching person as you."

And he looked up at her as she stood in front of him.

"You think so?" she said and placed the cigarette box she had been holding on a small table. "I don't."

"Aren't you rather well known here?"

"Excuse me?"

"I mean, don't you know many people?"

"No," she said. "Perhaps you have acquaintances everywhere."

"I don't recall having seen any. Regardless, there are two sorts of people. Those who know the whole world, and others, who are known to the whole world. I would still prefer belonging to the latter group."

She didn't answer right away. "And when," she finally asked, "did this Herr von So-and-So speak to you about me?"

"Yesterday afternoon."

"Already yesterday afternoon?"

"Yes. Aren't you familiar with someone else from my regiment in addition to Herr von Sodoma?"

"Not that I know of."

"It's all moot," he said. "I'd be more interested in who you are going out with. Must you go out with them?"

She looked at him for a long moment, then turned around, walked to the window and looked out into the courtyard. She stood on her left foot and moved the heel of her right foot up and down in her slipper. It was an unusually small and rosy heel.

"Well?" he asked.

She reached for a window wing, closed it, then tested the mechanics of the old fashioned brass handle. The she opened the window again, came back and sat on the divan next to Wallmoden.

"Listen," she said, "what did you tell him?"

"Whom?"

"This person with whom you talked about me."

"Herr von Baumgarten? I told him everything I knew about you."

"What you know about me?"

"Yes. Nothing."

"Why nothing?"

"Or as good as nothing. You had told me a few things, but I don't know if you were referring to yourself. You might have been speaking about a completely different person..."

"What does that mean?" She interrupted him and it seemed as though she were suppressing anger.

"One can only accept all this if one knows the person," he said. "But I don't know you. Your two marriages mean nothing to me. I listened to you as one would to a stranger. Your experiences would have told me far more if I knew you even a little better. When people really know each other there is perhaps nothing worse than sharing details from their past lives. Yes, I believe that the envy of the past is the most painful. What is past is past, but it is therefore also irrevocable. One can at least attempt to correct what is or what will be. Only the past is completely uncorrectable. It is, and remains, even embarrassingly in a certain way, a part of the present. For example, among all her men, a woman still feels only betrayed by her immediate lover.

"One should also add that that which is missed cannot be recaptured. To have omitted sins is probably the only true sin. One finds it so difficult not to always have had the woman one loves, and it is horrible to see the conviction with which people continue to miss everything.

"In short, it seems in reality we can only interest ourselves in people who haven't done anything unpleasant, but could do it at any time, or rather – that for their sake we do it to ourselves. It is amazing how much of pleasure is made up by displeasure. Anyway, there cannot be anything more boring than the secure love life of a Turk."

She had listened to him intently. Her sudden movement was as if she had taken in a breath.

"I think you overestimate things," she said.

"What things?"

"Well, love affairs, actually."

"It is strange. Just recently someone told me I overestimate death. Now you tell me I overestimate life. Let's move on! You are right. There really is no reason to argue about feelings which are only there to remind us that we didn't have them at the start."

"What do you mean?"

"One can't expect anyone to fall in love immediately. One actually only falls in love after the fact."

With these words his face moved to hers. With parted lips she breathed a kiss into his mouth. But when he wanted to take her into his arms, she pushed him away.

"What did you really tell Herr von Baumgarten?" she asked.

"At any rate, nothing he wanted to know."

"What did he want to know?"

"Many things I don't know myself. What the letter said, for example."

"What letter?"

"The one I took to Herr von Oertel."

"You told him about that?"

"Yes."

"Why? For what reason?"

"Because someone saw my car in the Piaristengasse. Frankly, he wanted to know what I was doing there."

"How did he come to ask you that?"

"Maybe he wanted to find out if you live there."

"But what concern is that of his?"

"You seem to be of the notion..."

"Yes?"

"...that it does concern him."

"What do you mean?"

"Listen," he said after a pause, "do you know – with the exception of Sodoma and me – anyone else in my regiment?"

"No, certainly not."

"But you seem to be known."

"That may be possible," she said, "if Sodoma talked about me. But what could he have said? I haven't known him any longer than you."

"But you already knew his wife."

"Yes, and ...?"

"Perhaps she told him something about you."

"What would she know about..."

"What did you speak to her about?"

"Nothing of importance. You heard it."

"And earlier? Before we arrived?"

"What women talk about."

He lit a new cigarette. "When did you come to Vienna?" he asked.

"Only recently."

"And before? Where did you live?"

"Tell me," she demanded, "what this Baumgarten really said about me!"

"Nothing." said Wallmoden. "He really said nothing. He only wanted to know this and that."

"For what reason?"

"The reason," said Wallmoden, "must have been that someone told him about you. Don't you think someone could talk about you?"

"No."

"Haven't you ever done anything that was obvious enough so that people talked about it?"

"Yes. Every time someone found themselves interested in things that do not concern them. But I do not know any types like that here."

"At any rate," he said, "you appear to value the fact that no one knows what you do."

"Herr von Baumgarten must have given you that idea."

"How so?"

"Obviously in gratitude for having given him the idea to be interested in me."

"Me?"

"Yes, you. Be honest – didn't he only want to know what you were doing on the Piaristengasse? That is all he was curious about. What cause did you have to tell him about me?"

"What do you mean by cause?"

"You are very foolish. You were used."

"How did he use me?"

"Maybe he didn't use you – but you used me."

"I wouldn't know how. If you really didn't want me to say anything then you should have let me know. Anyway, aren't you responsible for what you do?"

"Not necessarily."

"Well then, you see," he mumbled, "it is gossip."

"No, it would not have been gossip. But you can credit yourself for having started it."

He did not understand the major change the conversation had taken. Did this woman truly believe she could continually hide her existence? Perhaps she had not been this way for long.

"Listen," he said, "why do you imagine that Baumgarten was not interested in you but in this Oertel, about whom I said nothing? It is evident that you are more attractive to Baumgarten, since he continually asked about you and not at all about him. "

"Exactly."

"What exactly?"

"Oh," she cried, "you don't understand it!"

"Actually," he said, "I admit that. But it is laughable that we are arguing about a situation even he believed might be a misunderstanding."

"Then he would have also considered what would not have been a misunderstanding."

"No, he said nothing about that. I think there is no reason for us to continue to discuss this. I'd rather you'd confess why you want to abandon me tonight."

"I will guard myself from confessing anything more to you."

"I am only here because of you."

She looked at him. "Do you really believe," she said, "that you care about me? I am only asking because then the trouble you have already caused me might be a bit more understandable."

"I would be desolate," he said and reached for her hands, "if I had done that. But you don't think that it is really unimportant to consider what kind of reputation you have with a person you don't even know? What kind of a woman would you be, if you only did something or didn't do something with regard to your reputation. The reputation one has is nothing more than the opinion of others. Such an opinion is ultimately of no importance!"

"But one doesn't always live for the ultimate."

"There are times," he said," in which daily life behaves as if it

were ending. And if one considers that one might have to die –
in reality, those are the times in which one really lives."

With this he grasped her shoulders and pulled her to him.
Dusk had begun and the evening wind rustled the garden on the
other side of the courtyard. The air that now passed through the
windows was cooler. It was as if the autumn wind were blowing
across the countryside.

Traces of cigarette smoke swam across the darkening room.
In this silvery fog which swirled around the furniture, the face of
the young woman shimmered in a passive white, which felt like
the petals of a white bloom to the touch. She returned his kisses,
but kept her eyes set on him and without blinking, looking at
him as closely as possible. Tears forced her to only half-close her
lids, but never did she allow the fringes of these lids to block her
stare, which also never disclosed what she saw. She did not stop
Wallmoden from feeling her breasts through the silk she wore.
They only filled a gentleman's hand; one of the many breasts of
beautiful women that has always filled the hands of gentlemen.
Still, Wallmoden could not escape the feeling that she had her
limits, set by self-conscious thoughts, and there was no way
beyond these. At this particular moment, she set a silent, even
brooding defense against him. He was convinced she was
thinking about something else. This wordless coming to grips
lasted about half an hour. Thereafter she broke from him and
said she had to dress.

She hoped he would leave. But because he remained sitting
and sulking and lit a cigarette, she stepped behind a screen and
turned on a light. The room had become dark in the meantime.
The lamp filled the room with a rosy fog. He heard a cabinet
open and close. She threw a few items over the edge of the
screen.

"Well?"

He finally took in her voice. "Pardon me?" he asked.

"Why did you suddenly stop talking altogether?"

His voice had something akin to an amused tone. She also moved with intentional animation behind the screen.

"I am happy to see that you are in a good mood," he answered.

"You think so?"

"It is strange," he said, "what a good mood women are in when they didn't do what they should have."

"Yes," she laughed, "it is almost as if we had done something we shouldn't have."

"Don't laugh," he said.

She stepped out from behind the screen fastening the counterpart to the pearl drop shimmering on her right ear, onto her left. She wore an evening dress. The undersides of her arms glowed.

"Actually," she said, "I am not in as good a mood as you think. Above all, I am sorry that you are sulking. If you really don't know what to do with yourself tonight, come along."

"It's not about not knowing what to do," he replied, "it's that I wanted to spend the evening with you."

"Well then."

"But now you are already in evening dress. Last time I wore riding boots and now I am in a suit. It is really odd that I never manage to match you."

"It doesn't matter."

"And who are these people we are to meet?"

"If you are really coming along, I will ring them up," she said. "Are you coming?"

He shrugged. She seemed to take it as an affirmation. She left the room and he heard her on the telephone in the foyer. After a brief time she returned.

"We can go," she said and emptied the contents of a leather handbag into one of brocade. She reached for her coat. It was the same white one she wore the last time.

Wallmoden put out his cigarette and stood up.

"So you really mean," He said, "that..."

"Yes," she replied. "We are expected."

She handed him the coat. He kissed her neck as he hung it on her shoulders. She remained unfazed, looking forward. Only her shoulder blades softly moved, like the wings of a bird folding into rest.

5

"Did you bring your car?" she asked as they stepped out of the building.

"Yes," he said. "But I parked it on the Marokkanergasse. No one needs to know where I am."

They took a few steps in silence. The wind was still rushing through the garden. The scent from the branches, already a bit like autumn, mixed with the scent of the young woman. The heels of her shoes clattered on the irregular pavement. Her coat billowed. Under the flickering light of the street lanterns it seemed as if shadows were slipping by.

"To the Stallburggasse," she said as they got into the car.

"I have given up asking about the people we are meeting," he said.

"A certain Baron Drska," she said, "who has invited a few people to dinner."

"At his home?"

"Yes."

"Then why are you so secretive? One could almost truly believe you have no secrets."

"And I don't have any."

As they arrived at the Stallburggasse they began to study the buildings they were passing. "Here," she said and pointed to the entrance of a building with a balcony over the driveway, a dark façade and white window frames. "And you can just leave your car here. You don't need to drive it onto the Dorotheergasse."

"But to the Graben," he said, "because I can't park it here."

They deposited the vehicle and returned on foot. The entry gate was open. The driveway into the building was paved with wood and by the courtyard, ended by a glass wall. At his post a porter was reading a newspaper by a green and white enamel lamp with a glass shade. Over the staircase, which had unusually flat steps, gas lanterns were burning. A dolphin provided the handle to the door at which they rang.

A servant opened it and led them into a salon of white, dark red and some gold. A large crystal chandelier burned brightly. They were greeted by a good looking, perhaps a bit portly man of about fifty, undoubtedly the aforementioned host, as well as by a few other people including a young, strangely unfinished creature by the name of Cilly, whose hands and feet were too big for her body in a childlike way. Observing her, one naturally wondered what she would be like when she aged. The final guest, an Italian – the Principe Baraville-Septinguerra – entered, dressed in a double-breasted, ivory colored fresco smoking jacket. Wallmoden regretted that he had not actually been invited and that he now appeared in street dress. Drska mentioned it was a party nevertheless and offered him cigarettes. They were Simon Arzt.

There was no opportunity to exchange more than a few words because dinner was served immediately. The dining room was papered in green and was rather dark. Cuba and Cilly were the only women present. In addition to Drska, Wallmoden and Septinguerra, there were two others: one very quiet and unimposing gentleman referred to as "Herr President" and another, younger man, with tanned skin and eyebrows that grew together. He was wearing black trousers and a wine colored evening jacket with a shawl collar. The "President's" jacket was made of white linen. But it was so thickly woven and so strong, and the cut of the jacket was so fine, even if outmoded, that it was not hard to assume that the maker of this garment was a first-class, even an extraordinary tailor. Wallmoden thought it amusing to imagine that it had been created by legendary shopkeepers, such as the tailor to Edward VII, or someone of similar rank. There have always been individuals who have considered their tailors to be demigods (and vice versa). At any rate, it was a romantic notion to believe that a remnant of the excellence of a bygone world had been preserved with this garment, which was unmatched and which fit with a so-called hermetic comfort over the slender shoulders of the President. A man of his years no longer accepts transformation. He has found peace, he and the linen of his jacket, which, like the wood that continues to settle in the walls, then finally becomes still.

What are all these people doing here in all this exotic finery, thought Wallmoden. Why are they not in the country this summer? If he had not intended to remain unseen in Cuba's company by his squadron leader, he would have regretted that Kaufmann was missing this. The meal and the wines were superb. The conversations, particularly between Septinguerra and Drska, who was dressed in a white, embroidered vest, dominated the table and were quite animated. English was spoken for the sake of the Prince. It appeared that the host arranged hunting parties, mostly in Hungary, usually with the inclusion of Hungarian noblewomen. As a foreigner, Septinguerra was the exception and repeatedly spoke of the shooting of Polish bisons and did not care for such an inclusion. Wallmoden was puzzled that Drska even considered the issue of the bison. Nevertheless, he didn't immediately dismiss it.

There was a game reserve in Poland that belonged to the state and was not leased for private use. Drska mentioned that bison from this area passed back and forth to the neighboring reserves, so that one could, given certain conditions, have a shot at them.

"We could attempt to rent the neighboring reserve," he said.

"But you wouldn't have any luck," replied Wallmoden. "The bison are state property even in a neighboring private reserve, and one cannot obtain permission to hunt them."

"By that time," said Drska, "perhaps so."

"By when?"

"I simply don't understand," remarked Cuba, "what sort of pleasure this would be for you, Prince Septinguerra. Perhaps you would find a target, but only with a telescope and at four hundred paces. You might just as well shoot at a sparrow."

"I fear you really don't quite understand it, Cuba," said Drska. "For example, if one loves, one is not indifferent to what type of woman one has fallen for – aside from the fact that it may be a woman – to put it in your terminology – whom no one has taken a shot at."

Pistohlkors was a bit embarrassed by these words in a way that Wallmoden had not expected of a person, who, although still young, had been married twice and did not have a good reputation. It could, however, be that she was uncomfortable with Drska's turn of phrase. She threw a hasty glance at Cilly, but the young girl was laughing without restraint at something funny. Although she tried her best to stop it, Cuba found herself blushing uncontrollably.

"You might yet be correct, Baroness," declared the President, who appeared to be duty-bound to help Cuba out of this spot. "I myself have once" – he made a vague hand gesture – "hosted a hunt that cost me a half-million a year and was only done for the pleasure of my guests. I had to offer something to the people I was associated with but – believe it or not – I have never hunted.

"One day however, as I passed between two fields, I found myself five paces from a rabbit. One of my guests I was accompanying placed his weapon in my hands. It was a fine shotgun, with barrels made by Purdey, as I recall. The rabbit was probably not as surprised as I was by this gun. It was the only time I had ever attempted to shoot game. I used to practice pistol shooting in my free time, and I dare say, I could still shoot the ace out of a card at ten to fifteen paces. The rabbit was a complete failure though. I missed him by a wide margin."

Wallmoden leaned forward to hear the voice of the elderly man, which, although soft, was very penetrating. After a moment he straightened up.

"Actually," Wallmoden commented, "that is quite odd. I had a cousin who was a wonderful marksman, at least years ago and... oh, have you heard of him?" he asked as the President nodded. "You knew him? Anyway, he was of the mind that a shot, once it has left the pistol, has such a precarious balance that it is subject to the tiniest influences, and the most unnoticeable. Human will, for example. And not just from the marksman, but also from the target. He didn't reach this conclusion completely on his own, but gained it from a very strange source, from an Englishman whom he... well, frankly, whom he shot in Spa."

"Yes," said the President. "I know. The event earned great attention at a time already rich enough in sensationalism."

"The reasons that led to the duel," Wallmoden added after a moment, "are not appropriate for discussion here."

"Why aren't they appropriate?" the President asked with a smile.

"It is simply not a pleasant subject for discussion," answered Wallmoden, who didn't quite understand what he meant. "Anyway, it is possible that my cousin's, or rather his adversary's theory may be correct. There are people, so called mediums, who can move things without touching them, by force of sheer will and sometimes against their will. They can sit in a room, and after a while the things on the table or the things around them will move towards them. Stones even fly through the air... This is of course so well known it is hardly worth talking about. So when a thing that rests can be moved in this manner, imagine how much easier it is to influence things that are already in such an unstable condition – like a flying bullet. A parallelogram would display the original path against the influencing power resulting in a corrected path... In actuality, this is much more complicated. Two high curves and a line that is actually a curve as well. But I don't want to bore you with this. My cousin elaborated that otherwise one couldn't explain why many marksmen often hit targets which, due to their small size, go unnoticed. Conversely, this would lead to an explanation why relatively large targets are often missed.

"I recall that during the first days on the front, I often left our trench to go for a walk in a nearby forest. There was a path that led through a particular hollow, where a dead toad had lain for several days.

"Because I was revolted by this toad, I left the hollow and made my way to the forest on the upper rim of the path. I didn't feel completely safe because I could not see the Russian position from the hollow. Only the tops of their trees were discernible.

"On my way through the hollow, I heard nearby an often soft but unusually repetitious clattering, which I couldn't explain. I would repeatedly stop and inspect the ground around me. I never discovered anything there nor far away. I never saw anyone. I was alone and the rather ghostly clattering continued on. I can hardly explain how ugly this sound was. I can only say that it was the most disturbing sound I have ever heard.

"Now, I know that death, if it had a sound, must have one like that. I had no idea that the sounds around me were shots. There had been increasing fatalities among those who crossed the hollow, and it turned out that they had not been shots from the Russian camp, but from the tree tops, where their sharpshooters sat. The bullets were barely audible. Perhaps they had been shot from guns calibrated for small targets.

"Later I also learned to distinguish all different kinds of fire, but I never again heard a sound even similar to the sound of those shots *before* I knew they were shots. The strangest thing is that these telescopic riflemen, so-called snipers, did not hit me. It is certainly puzzling because I often stood in the hollow for minutes, looking around and listening. I may not have been shot because I did not want to be shot."

All had listened attentively. Then he added: "Obviously the Englishman who gave my cousin his theory did not want to escape the deadly bullet. His seconds later explained that he believed in his views and predicted his own death. He was a major in the British army, the younger brother of a certain Lord Winter. He had explained with precision why my cousin must shoot him with such an imprecise thing as a dueling pistol. It may have been that his life was over. One should mention that after having killed him, my cousin never again touched a pistol!"

"Which is to say that only the true artist doesn't value his own art," remarked Drska, and led the way into dinner.

After the meal there were games. The covered up windows were now open because Drska complained that it had become suffocatingly hot. Wallmoden considered this irresponsible but resisted making any sort of comment.

At first he lost, but then he won a sizable amount. Had he won first, then lost, he could have surmised he was in the grasp of swindlers. This way it was the opposite – or it seemed to be the opposite. Originally, he did not want to play at all. Drska convinced him to do so for the sake of Septinguerra and the President, who would be happy if he did. The President led such an isolated life that these dinners and the occasional gathering were his only diversions.

"Had you counted on me?" asked Wallmoden.

"Since we knew that you would come – yes," said Drska.

(The President played in a unique but sympathetic a manner. His stakes were, at least at the start, not very high. Nevertheless, he often made high bets with the same composure he had with the very small bets. In many ways it was as if he weren't playing for money at all, but simply to be polite. Wallmoden had the impression that he could not be very wealthy. But whoever was once rich will never be completely poor. He would know that money does not matter, but rather the by-products of money.)

Meanwhile, Cuba entertained herself with the young man in the wine-colored jacket whose name was something like Simay or Schimay, and with Cilly. The three of them sat somewhat apart on a satin sofa, drinking and smoking.

When, after some time had passed, Wallmoden looked in their direction again, they were gone. Nor did they return. Cuba's absence – especially the fact that she had disappeared with the other two – disturbed Wallmoden greatly. Failing to calm himself, he suddenly dropped his cards, stood, and mumbled that he must be excused for a short while.

He did not understand his agitation. He stepped into the next room – the salon in white and dark red – then into the room where they had dined. It was dark and the table had already been cleared. In the two adjoining rooms – a yellow salon and a hunting room, a sort of trophy gallery – there was no one. The apartment seemed very large and reached far into the rear part of the building. Wallmoden arrived at a bedroom, obviously that of the inhabitant, and tripped on a pair of slippers which stood in front of the bed on a bear rug. In the dim light he noticed there were also unfurnished rooms which did not even have windows. In a hallway, which ran parallel with the courtyard, he thought he had found the kitchen door. Wallmoden heard the servants talking. The hallway came to an end at a far door behind which someone was coughing. After a moment, Wallmoden knocked. Since there was no further sound, he knocked even harder the second time.

Scuffling steps neared the door and it opened. An old, hunched over man in a brocade robe and slippers looked out. Behind him there was a dimly lit bedroom overcrowded with furniture, paintings and objects.

A woman whose gray-haired head was only visible lay in bed and asked what was happening.

"Who are you?" Wallmoden demanded of the old man.

Stunned, the old man mentioned his name but Wallmoden did not understand. "Shut the door!" shouted the woman in bed, to which the old man stepped into the hall and closed the door behind him.

"Do you live here?" inquired Wallmoden.

"Yes," said the old man, "we live here now."

"I thought Baron Drska lives here."

"He lives in front. He has been living here for one week."

"Why?"

"Because it is his apartment," answered the old man, looking at him askance, in a birdlike way. Wallmoden heard the kitchen door behind him. The servants – the butler and two young women – having heard the confrontation, peered out from the kitchen. Wallmoden realized he would not know how to explain his presence here and why he was asking so many questions that had no actual purpose. Just then a bell rang, and the butler made his way through the hall to the front of the apartment.

Wallmoden left the old man and followed the butler, who stepped through a side door as Wallmoden continued on, and found himself in the trophy room again, the dining room, the two salons, back in the game room.

They had stopped playing. Cuba, however, had not returned. Nevertheless, Wallmoden did not want to inquire about her. He had already decided to bid his farewell without much fuss, when the door opened and two civilian-clothed police inspectors followed by several policemen in uniform were led by the two servants into the room.

Of course, thought Wallmoden. This is the result! The others did not seem particularly disconcerted. Smoking a cigar from a paper holder, Drska was not disturbed in the least. He stared at the party, one arm hanging over the chair's back, his legs crossed.

The officers requested those present to identify themselves. With the exception of Wallmoden, all had foreign passports. Drska tossed his passport carelessly, and it seemed to Wallmoden even somewhat scornfully, onto the table. Septinguerra offered his with aplomb, as if he were certain that his country would make the police answer for this interruption.

As a matter of fact, the passports did not fail to make an impression on the officers. They studied the passport of the President, who was Hungarian, and asked to have some words translated. When asked what his profession is, the President gave an odd reply: professor.

"What is this gathering about?" asked one of the officers.

"It is what you see," answered Drska, pointing to the card table with his cigar tip. Wallmoden could not understand why no one had at least tried to disrupt the cards. Drska, however, regarded these cards with a certain sense of satisfaction.

"What sort of game is this?" asked the officer.

"Examine for yourself."

"Ecarté?"

Drska nodded. The detectives seemed disappointed. They began to search the entire apartment and requested that the party accompany them. Wallmoden had to visit all the rooms he had already seen, as well as a few he had not previously discovered. The old couple was disturbed again. It was revealed that they were the actual owners of the apartment and Drska had merely rented rooms from them.

Wallmoden saw no trace of Cuba, Cilly and the certain Herr

Schimay. After about three-quarters of an hour, the detectives left with their people.

"Forgive the disturbance, Count Wallmoden," said Drska, and glanced at the match that lit a new cigar. "But you had lost interest in playing regardless."

"Not really," said Wallmoden.

"I do not believe this matter will have any repercussions."

"How do you know that?"

"Well," considered Drska, "it just appears that way to me. Anyway, I am very grateful to the gentlemen."

"What for?"

"For their kindness."

With that, the evening, which was hardly old, seemed to have found its end. Wallmoden left with Septinguerra, who was cursing, and the President, who remarked that it was pointless to change oneself.

"Do come back again soon," said Drska. Wallmoden left the other two at the entrance to the building.

As he walked along, he tried to convince himself that his irritation was insignificant. In actuality, he found himself tangled in a net of events he did not understand and could no longer escape.

6

He was also unable to control his desire to see Cuba again. Around noon on Saturday he simply surrendered. He took leave until midnight Sunday, got into his car and drove to Vienna, "to see the person who had so rudely left Drska's party without saying good-by." He chose not to imagine a specific reason for her action. The face of Herr Schimay, however, continued to force itself into his thoughts, a man who had spoken with no one except Cuba all evening; and the visage of Cilly, the girl with the large extremities, who became more repugnant the more he thought of her. The strangest thing was Drska's silence regarding the disappearance of the three – although he may have been influenced by the arrival of the police. Or perhaps he had his mind on other things.

Wallmoden arrived in Vienna around three p.m. The countryside appeared to stretch far into the city that day. One could even imagine being in a suburb on the Mariahilfer Strasse. The city was built on the form of several outlying areas around a center that had disappeared. A wave of late summer flooded the streets. People wandered as if on forgotten pathways.

The Schwarzenberg Palace seemed to be out in the country, like an estate somewhere in Bohemia. Pigeons and dust swirled in the air. Vehicles rattled down the Rennweg, but the Salesianergasse was deserted. A whitish sunlight burned on the pavement. A dog, which may have been sleeping in the shade, ran barking after the car as if it were angry at having been awakened. His mouth moved with the pointless spasms of an old man's jaw. When Wallmoden stopped, the dog continued to run as if it had totally forgotten the vehicle. Yawning, he disappeared into the Strohgasse.

In front of a dairy, children were playing. One of them, a boy of about four, left his comrades and was crying. His face was completely red with torment. His legs were bent and he stepped on the outside rim of his bare feet and extended his large toe upwards as if he were wearing shoes that were too tight. In addition, the trousers on this stubborn image were unfastened and spanned across his belly like a drum. He wandered off, embittered to the point of squealing. What was happening here? thought Wallmoden. Why this rage in an empty street? A man with two horses came out of the opposite driveway. The horses were already harnessed. They were old and might have belonged to a transport worker. Even the harnesses were old, but the blinders still had closed crowns on them. There were still many private stalls in this area. These people had all once owned their own coaches. Now, one hardly ever saw a horse. It was strange to see them being walked. It was as if the heat had forced out things that were no longer visible.

Wallmoden glanced through the window into the courtyard as he climbed the stairs to Cuba's apartment. A tree rustled in the garden. It had peculiar, overly thin ash-type leaves and vine-like branches. They stood in panicles and trembled at the slightest motion in the air. The stone steps of the staircase smelled of cleaning fluid. On every floor there was a water main. The faucets dripped. It was as if the drops divided time he no longer believed existed, into equal intervals.

He rang. As he tried to enter, however, he was told Cuba was not at home. He had difficulty hiding his disappointment. He asked where she might be, but that was not known.

It was not clear whether the person who opened the door was

the maid or the owner of the apartment. She had opened the door the previous time Wallmoden was here, yet he did not think about this then. She wore an old embroidered dress, had bare legs and was wearing a pair of well-worn shoes. She might have been a woman who was underdressed because she was at home or a girl who was in the midst of dressing to go out.

Wallmoden asked if Cuba hadn't said where she was going.

No, she did not say, answered the person.

Wallmoden wanted to know when she had left.

"At noon," she replied. "Didn't you arrange for a meeting with her?"

No, answered Wallmoden. Not really. When would Cuba be back?

In a few days perhaps.

Not for a few days?

Yes. She looked at him. Her back was leaning against a foyer cabinet. She had pulled together the folds of her dress as if it were a morning robe, and as she turned the heel of her foot back and forth, she dug the point of her foot into the floor.

"And didn't she say where she was going either?"

"No."

After a moment, Wallmoden stepped into the foyer. Then he went to Cuba's room, opened the door and glanced into the room. The person closed the apartment door and followed him.

Cuba's things were still lying about, so it did not seem as if she would be gone for very long. Wallmoden wandered about for a few moments, then sat on the divan.

"Did she go alone?" he asked.

"Yes," said the woman. "Naturally."

"Didn't she take anything with her?"

"Of course. A few things."

She obviously considered it pointless to have a long discussion about this matter – Cuba was gone. She seemed to consider speaking completely superfluous, and just stood there and stared at him. Her hands no longer grasped the folds of her dress, they simply hung, empty, and she just stood there. Her mouth bore the trace of a smile. It took Wallmoden a few moments to comprehend what she meant. That Cuba wasn't here was obvious. It was that kind of afternoon. When people are away they are gone, and it is as if they had never been there. When someone comes, they are simply here, and one does not need to understand why they are here. On this particular afternoon, in which Wallmoden imagined that time no longer existed, it was a time as good as any other, but it was only ever just a moment long. There was nothing before it and nothing beyond it.

He stood. It was as if he were existing in two events in which one continued and one remained static. Actually, it was as if he were living in two people. He moved toward the woman and kissed her on the mouth. He felt her breasts through her dress. They were like two hard objects sewn into the material. She spoke: "Don't do that." He had two independent trains of thought at the very same time. While one of the two people concentrated on her, the other thought about the room, so to speak, searching for a letter that Cuba might have left behind, disclosing where she was – or at least a note. And as if he had indeed found it, this note, he reached for his hat and gloves and left the woman standing there – standing with an arm over her eyes and backed up against the wall between two windows, wondering about the vagueness of this man from the so-called upper classes. But even the simplest young people –she thought – often display shockingly irregular behavior.

He drove immediately to a shoemaker who had been recommended to him, as if it were of the utmost urgency, and ordered a pair of riding boots with double cork soles, a toe of Russian leather and a leg of calf. He also paid immediately.

Thereafter he took a deep breath as if he had accomplished something that – and he had no idea why – could not be postponed.

The boots would be ready in eight days. I should have already ordered them on Tuesday, he thought to himself. Nevertheless, it's good that I at least ordered them now. Who knows when they will really be ready?

Finally, he asked the shoemaker if he might use the telephone, and he called Drska. Drska wondered why Cuba hadn't told anyone where she was going, and after a moment he said he believed she was in Baden.

The first thing Wallmoden saw in Baden was Oertel, who was sleeping in a lounge chair in the garden of a hotel.

Wallmoden stopped his car, got out and woke Oertel.

Oertel seemed pleased to see Wallmoden. "You can see how bored I am here," he remarked, pointing to himself as if he were indicating some pitiable object.

"Nevertheless," he added, "I am convinced that your visit is not to see me, but to see our young lady friend."

"Right again," said Wallmoden. "But this time it was easy to guess. I had no idea that *you* would also be here."

"Actually," said Oertel, "it is fairly easy to surmise the circumstances. The difficulty arises only in estimating the actions of others. They always act a tad sillier than oneself. And it usually reveals itself to have been the wiser action."

"You are a wonder," said Wallmoden. "You wake from a deep sleep and already say something of profound truth."

"That is no compliment," answered Oertel. "At least not for truth. I think that the way women awake, for example, is far more exciting. They usually tell an untruth."

"The lady," asked Wallmoden, "whom you call our young friend, is she here?"

"Certainly. Did you have difficulty in finding out? I reproach myself for not having informed you. That she did not inform you was predictable."

"Why was it predictable?"

"Didn't you have your own reasons to believe so?"

"No," said Wallmoden. "What do you mean?"

"Oh," said Oertel, "she is just that way. Actually a very shy person, you know. It is strange how we perceive women to be so similar, and how different they are from one another in reality. Sometimes two women live under the same roof and after trying to win one without success, the other is happily yours. One simply never knows why."

Wallmoden looked at him.

"It is particularly so with Cuba, I mean Baroness Pistohlkors," added Oertel. "I believe I mentioned to you already that we have known each other for some time. She is the most decent person in the world, but lately she has had the odd proclivity of being with other women who – let us just say – have hardly been her equal in moral quality. I don't consider myself particularly attractive, but I have had difficulty with the often sudden interest of her girlfriends, even so far as extricating myself from the advances of her boarders."

Wallmoden didn't know what to say. He was speechless. It seemed clear that this man – and perhaps Cuba as well – were responsible for the circumstances in which he found himself this afternoon in the Salesianergasse.

"One can, however, not say that she did not consider her reputation," added Oertel. "On the contrary, perhaps she wanted to underscore it by associating with her opposites. It can also be that she hadn't given her reputation, in which she is secure, a single thought. It is usually the most respectable women, as opposed to others, who are indulgent in a manner we do not understand. Yes, they are often the 'chance encounter' directors and matchmakers for their sisters, perhaps because of a desire for adventure they cannot justify having themselves, or perhaps even because of an envy-tinged fascination with the temperaments of others. Perhaps she wants her surroundings to make up for all that she has omitted in her own life. Because catching up – which is how she often presents herself – is how it will have to be. Isn't it peculiar that one can deny and value something so fervently at the very same time? The only similarity would be the constant admission of a weakness."

"Listen," said Wallmoden, "and you will forgive me, especially after what you just said, but the Baroness does not seem to me to have the best reputation."

"Yes," answered Oertel, "I have already heard that this is what you think."

"Really? From whom did you hear this?"

"From the Baroness herself."

"From her?"

"Absolutely. Nevertheless, I ask you to believe me that she is respectability personified. Your hair would probably stand on end if you knew just *how* respectable she is."

"Very nice," said Wallmoden, who had decided not to believe anything anymore.

"But without doubt, you will want to see her now," said Oertel.

"You mean ...?"

"Exactly."

"I fear you haven't guessed it so completely this time," mumbled Wallmoden.

"But of course. Whatever a man might think of a woman, he will never give her up until he has what he wants from her. Women know that. It is therefore even more surprising that they let men achieve anything at all. One shouldn't credit so much spirit to creatures whose passion is in the bargain."

And with that, he rose from the chaise and shook his trousers into order. "Let us go," he said.

"Isn't she staying here?" asked Wallmoden.

"No. She declined that. Not that she would disdain staying at the same hotel out of prudery, but frankly, I am still a bit in love with her, and she was concerned that she might still have an effect on me."

The evening that Wallmoden spent in the company of Oertel, Cuba and an elderly lady, a Frau Terharen, whom Cuba was visiting, was hideous. It began with Cuba's embarrassment upon seeing Wallmoden – whether this was because of the situation she left for him at her apartment, or because of some other reason was not apparent. But the following day was hardly more pleasant. Cuba's embarrassment, rigidity and self-consciousness became intolerable. She even refused to change when they all went to the sulfur baths. Fully attired in hat, stockings and shoes, she sat under a large umbrella in the sweltering heat. Oertel, and to Wallmoden's particular dismay, also Frau Terharen, seemed to be most amused by the situation. After dinner on Sunday, as Wallmoden indignantly suggested he had to leave, Oertel conveyed a surprising bit of news.

Wallmoden had already said his good-byes to the ladies, who had returned to their rooms. He had finally tried to coax Cuba into telling him why she had left Drska's party. All he obtained was Cuba's reticent explanation that she had been tired.

"Listen," said Oertel, as he accompanied Wallmoden to his car, "she is simply in love with you. Haven't you noticed?"

"Don't be ridiculous!" said Wallmoden. "Or don't make me ridiculous, whichever you please."

"No," said Oertel, "she really is in love with you. She was once with me and acted in the same way. But I hope you imagine as little as I did then – that this could mean anything at all."

"What should it mean?"

"Well, what it would mean with every woman, or at least with most other women. She is probably sitting up in her room at this very minute turning her heart into a murder pit."

"A... what is she making of her heart?"

"I don't know," said Oertel. "You are aware that she has already been married twice."

"Yes, she told me about it."

"Well, she does that often. I think she does it so no one will imagine the opposite."

"The opposite of what?"

"How do I say this as tactfully as possible?" said Oertel. "They were marriages in name only."

"In name only... "

"Yes. And I also think that the many men who were in love with her and didn't marry her had better luck than her so-called husbands."

"It's impossible!" replied Wallmoden. "How do you know all this?"

"Oh," said Oertel, "it's pretty well known – and she herself finds it necessary, to her embarrassment, to admit it."

"She told me she divorced her first husband because of an argument over a brush, and her second husband died because he was so thin that the European climate didn't agree with him!"

"Well," said Oertel, as he made a face, "she never really cared much for thin men. It's as if she wanted to compensate for her exaggerated ideals regarding the weakness of her soul... But who dares to ridicule her! Perhaps the soul of this woman, who is actually a girl, is no less beautiful in its substance than her admittedly wonderful body. Perhaps on those long legs of hers she is offering the buds of her breasts, the unopened blossom of her mouth, like long-stemmed roses to someone who will never come to take her. Perhaps all the trivialities with which she defends her situation are no less important than the very pride of a soul. Perhaps the physical complications are, in truth, the only opportunity for us to notice the soul.

"At any rate, it is no glory for a woman to be as tepid as most others. But not to be able to love is almost as great as eternal love. What glory there is when one cannot love, and does! Perhaps it is simply the fate of this woman that no one can awaken her from this spell, or undo it, like a belt. If people who have almost always found each other by accident, fall in love, then all her love, as great as it is, is nothing but accidental. Her love is probably not meant to be an accident. She is probably not satisfied with the shallowness of an accidental meeting like all the others, who then give their heart to such an accident. Perhaps she waits in vain for a meeting that is not accidental. Perhaps it is even her fate never to have this meeting. There are certainly those who claim that there is no such thing as fate. But this is neither here nor there. It even seems to be very comfortable to deny it for a moment. But if one denies it, then everything becomes even more incomprehensible..."

Wallmoden listened, his foot already on the running board. But after a particular moment, he stopped listening. He turned and left suddenly.

With large steps he returned to the hotel and hurried up the stairs. The corridors were carpeted and his steps could not be heard. He turned the handle on Cuba's door and it yielded. He pushed it open.

Cuba stood in the center of the room, and as the door opened, she turned around. She gazed at him for only a moment, and one could tell by her eyes that she knew he had understood everything.

Her eyes were opened wide, and there was no trace of fear in them, only a realization that the moment had come, *her* moment. There was a suggestion of a smile on her lips, like someone who fears death, but at the moment of dying, because it is almost over, smiles.

He went to her without a word, took her in his arms and kissed her. Her arms first warded him off, then embraced him and she locked her lips for him in opening them. It was the truest passion of this woman whose devotion had been aversion.

"Come tomorrow," she whispered. "Don't stay tonight. Not now. I'll return to the city tomorrow. Come to me then. Come in the afternoon. I love you. *I will be waiting for you.*" There was a conviction in the tone, in the vibration of her voice, a complete certainty that what had to happen could not conceivably happen today, and that its very moment was not now, but must be at a different time, as if her entire life were nothing but the postponement of a time that was to come, and never did.

As he drove home, he was forced to take a detour, which took him nearly to Vienna and lasted two hours. The feelings of anticipation and happiness overtook him in the darkness of the car.

The streets, once lively, had now been emptied. The sprawl of the landscape shimmered, almost imperceptibly, in the reflection of the diamond dust scattered across the sky. The foliage of the woods hung like clouds. Mars shone through the left car window. It stood like a glowing spear point on the zenith. Eastward, there was a glassy glint, like the eye of a madman: Saturn had risen above the horizon.

The street lamps of the garrison town illuminated empty paths and squares. The haloes and rays of a memorial column were rigidly golden. The clocks of the church towers chimed, echoing brass through the darkness. As Wallmoden drove into the camp – it was shortly after midnight – he found the gate wide open and saw large shadows standing in rows against the buildings. They were the vehicles of the entire squadron. He was informed that the regiment would march in forty-five minutes.

7

The alarm had signaled thirty hours before, on Saturday afternoon, as Wallmoden had left the camp. They had attempted to find him in Vienna, to inform him, but he could not be found.

He found it difficult to take care of all his necessities within the allotted time he had left. Above all, the destination of the regiment was unclear. Into the field, advised Rosthorn, who was already prepared and kept Wallmoden company. But which field asked Wallmoden, who hardly believed it. Is there one? Apparently there was, said Rosthorn, who had been dressed and armed for hours to the point of no return. And if there weren't one, weren't a field, one would be made. He stood with his helmet on his head, in the center of the room under a lamp. The helmet threw a shadow on his face and mouth, out of which, like from the Cavern of Cumae, dark prophecies resounded.

Wallmoden took off his civilian clothing and put on his uniform – his only one. It had been, he thought, too late after all to order a second pair of boots. He should have ordered them immediately after Oertel suggested it. Oertel, as usual, had guessed correctly. Wallmoden's orderly appeared and pressed rations, a gasmask and Losantin tablets into his hands. These tablets were new to Wallmoden. What were they, he asked. Something against gas poisoning, explained Rosthorn. The so-called gas-tarpaulin would also be distributed. Wallmoden collected handfuls of material and stuffed it all into two packs, pulled the wool blanket off the bed and tossed it in as well. His orderly packed the ration pack to capacity. Wallmoden owned two coats, but realized he had no travel coat. All the cabinets were open, and the lamps illuminated a confusion of small objects that covered the table, chair and bed. Wallmoden packed his civilian clothes into a suitcase. What would happen to them, he asked. Rosthorn informed him that the suitcase could remain here. Reproachful like a god of war, for this tardy arrival, he avoided touching these articles of peace. Much still lay around the room. "Minima non curat praetor," explained Rosthorn.

Wallmoden tossed everything into a cabinet, added the suitcase and locked it. Then he drove his car into one of the garages and left it there. In the meantime, his orderly had loaded up his transport. The air was already filled with the noise of motors, and the darkness resounded like the inside of a stringed instrument invaded by a swarm of bees. The Fifth and Sixth Squadrons had already begun to move.

Wallmoden attempted to take in the entire event, but could not muster any clear thoughts. He was only able to continue his thoughts from an hour ago. He thought it would all continue as it had. Even his thoughts continued as they had. But his actions were completely different from his thoughts. He moved through the darkness and thought about Cuba. He saw the Salesianergasse before him, and simultaneously strapped his pistol on tighter. He again had the feeling of having dissolved into two beings with different ways. One had, as it were, not yet returned, and only merely considered nothing more than a temporary return. It had remained with the woman he had left – and to whom until now he had believed he would return. It was planning their tomorrow. The other being was consumed by the events that were taking him away. It was not planning anything. It had suddenly been awakened as if by the memory of the long-vanished morning air. The future was once again full of danger.

The Seventh Squadron drove up to its alarm station. "Well," said Kaufmann as Wallmoden entered, "nice to see you're here," and he held out his hand. In the meantime, the Eighth Squadron (heavy artillery) was also on the move. The cavalry support and the anti-tank cannons rolled up behind their battle wagons. The Seventh, and last squadron, also started up. It departed the camp through the "Porta Praetoria."

The streets echoed as they drove through the city. There were already people outside who were waving. They disappeared behind like shadows. The column rolled onto the highway. Behind this regiment, another had connected. The column was enormous. The rear lights shone into the horizon like a procession of pairs of red candles. The squadrons drove eastward.

Even Wallmoden sat next to his driver and drove eastward. He drove back on the same street which, an hour previously, he had driven westward. His car had been one of the very few on the road. He had come from the woman he loved. He had been certain that this road would only take him back to her. Now it was droning with army vehicles.

Once, when troops began to march, it was with the noise of countless hooves, as if the wind were blowing piles of dried leaves around, or as if ice castles were collapsing. Now motors thundered. But if once, when one had stood in the lines or right before the lines, one had thought that, together with the regiments, one was covering the landscape as if with unalterable geometric figures, in which, always and everywhere, one knew precisely at which position every individual stood, as if in a constellation: the eagles, the trumpeters, the officers, and in which the hermetic order would have upheld even a dead man – thus, one still felt the structure of this mutuality today, but it was a more terrible one than ever, and it was not only *with* the people but *in the community* of the people, from which there was no escape, that one moved against a threat. Against what threat?

One did not know. One never knows.

Strangely, Wallmoden did not seem to think he was driving anywhere other than to Cuba Pistohlkors. For some reason, he didn't believe the way could lead to anything other than her. At the same time, he told himself it was ridiculous to continue to avoid the truth. After all, he had been sitting in this wagon for almost an hour already. The men of the regiments – not only his, but of the others – marched. Nevertheless, the road could only always lead to her.

The battle wagons rolled on with constancy. The men slept. Some civilian vehicles that were returning late from the countryside overtook the convoy. There were even people who held bouquets of flowers they had picked, as if nothing had happened and as if nothing would happen. And the others, propped up on their guns, drove into the unknown. This co-existence was the strangest of all. But this co-existence always occurred.

Command wagons chased alongside the convoy. It moved northeasterly. At the crossing, in spotlights, the waiting motorcycles rattled. The convoy moved onto unpaved streets and began to cover itself in dust. As it passed through small towns, the shuttered windows of the houses stared back in blindness. At about three a.m. they crossed the Danube. The shadow of the willow trees bent over the pools of the river as if the dead had dipped their hair into the sad tides. The waters sparkled under the bridge.

Thereafter, the stars began to disappear from the sky. As if streams of mist had dropped from above, darkness descended. Only Saturn glimmered. It was now positioned on the blue-tinged zenith. The faces and bodies of the sleeping men were covered with a pale dust, which made them appear as if they were frozen bodies in the snow.

Between five and six o'clock they reached the Reichsstrasse, which led them in a northern direction from Vienna. They were allotted two hours of rest. The street became lively with farm vehicles. In the south, blocked by the mountains, the steam of the city brewed. The sun came up. Wallmoden thought, isn't this still the same day as yesterday? Around seven, the process continued. The convoy turned right. The paths taken were narrow; the wheels ground the dust. It rose in high clouds and covered the hilly terrain. The land of dust began here. It stretched to Hungary and into Poland, over an unending Russia to the place, just on the other side of Asia, where the land once again fell to the sea. It reached beyond borders. But it began here.

The morning became hot. The sun was beating down. The wind was hissing through the bushes that followed the course of the paths. The treeless hills were surging. In the area facing against the March, the squadrons began to take up quarters individually. At about ten o'clock, one was in Jedenspeigen. The village lay in a hollow over which the sky stood like a glistening glass bell. The squadron was drawn up in position in foot-deep dust before the castle. The men were accommodated in the village, and the officers in the castle.

Wallmoden retired to bed and slept until three in the afternoon. Then he arose, went to the window and looked out. All was quiet, only the working of a thrashing machine was perceptible from afar, and, once or twice, a rooster would crow. One was leaning at the window as if on a parapet. The slopes of the hill over against the windows were cultivated with beets. The distance stretched bluishly in a sad gleam.

Above the entrance to the castle he had read the plaque for a member of the Kollonitz family. Upon the wall of the courtyard, a sundial was painted, with transits of strangely painted constellations. In front of the building there was a triangular, overgrown garden. Plum trees grew by the walls.

Wallmoden began to consider what had actually happened and

what he should now do. It was three-fifteen. At five, five-thirty at the latest, he was to have been at Cuba's in Vienna. He considered the distance to be between fifty and sixty kilometers. But the city seemed to be more distant than the moon. And Kaufmann would inform him of this later: Vienna was now an impossibility. The regiment would probably move into Slovakia. This might happen very soon or at some point. At any rate, no one was allowed to leave the squadron. How would Wallmoden get to Vienna anyway, since he had left his car at the camp? With a tank perhaps?

The solution would have been to phone Vienna, but Wallmoden still did not know Cuba's number. Even the name of the woman with whom he had almost spent an exciting afternoon, and whose telephone it most likely was, remained unknown to him. This is what comes from being constantly persuaded that names are unimportant.

He decided to send a telegram and began to walk to the post office. He had to cross the town to get there. It consisted of one single street that lay in the afternoon heat. A dirty brook drudged across its middle. The houses were all similarly earthen. It already reminded one a bit of Hungary. It turned out later that the inhabitants did not speak Hungarian, but Czech.

Wallmoden telegraphed that he could not come and requested that she call him the following morning at eleven. A letter would follow. He wrote this letter upon his return to the castle. It wasn't a long letter, but he worked on it into the evening. He sat at the table and stared at the sheet of paper in front of him with an unaccountable sadness.

The sun set. It grew a bit cooler and in the west a crescent moon of dim light followed the sun with its silvery feet and stepped into a distant sea. They ate at the garden of an inn, which lay at the crossing of the town's main street with another that led to Duernkrut. Following Kaufmann's suggestion chickens had been ordered, which first had to be caught in the trees where they had gone to sleep. They drank a great deal. Between ten and eleven they went home in a mixture of starlight and the dust which their steps had raised. They had no idea where they were going. This feeling of stepping into the unknown did not leave Wallmoden, even in sleep.

That night he dreamt an unusual dream. It was strange because it was indistinguishable, or almost so, from waking reality. At least it was so because he had entered the dream without distinguishing it from reality. Wallmoden dreamt he was lying awake in his bed in which he was actually sleeping. He thought he heard steps approaching the door to his room. They were steps that came from the hall next to his room where the orderlies slept. The steps sounded insecure, as if a person were walking in the dark, and in truth, the hall would only be illuminated by starlight. The steps halted for a moment in front of the door, then the door opened slowly. Wallmoden sat up in bed to ask who it was, but he could not understand the reply. In the light of the stars that shone through the opened door, Wallmoden thought he recognized the outline of a woman's figure.

This figure entered and moved through the darkness toward the furnace where she immediately began to work on different controls. "What the devil is going on?" shouted Wallmoden, at which the woman became still, moved to the door and left the room. He heard her go through the hall and open another door. She left this one open as well. For a while, Wallmoden heard nothing else. It was silent and he was ready to get up and shut his door when he again heard footsteps. This time it was from two people. At the same moment, a ray of light came through the open door. The footsteps again approached and two women entered. One held a candle, the other, two buckets of water.

They seemed to be servants at the castle. One had black hair, the other was blond. One of the pair must have been the one here before, because the two moved to the furnace without the need for explanation. There they pulled out a flat wooden tub that had stood behind the furnace, and a screen. Wallmoden then heard them pouring the water from the buckets into the tub.

The candle stood behind the screen and Wallmoden saw by the projected shadows that the girls had started to undress. How nice, thought Wallmoden, the two want to take a bath! That people with whom he was billeted would often find odd hours to move or repair things was something he had gotten used to in the war. But people had never bathed in his room before. Well, he thought and laughed, times are changing and this is probably a sign of progress. "I don't wish to disturb the ladies," he said, but the ladies did not seem in the least to be disturbed. They had already disrobed, had stepped into the tub and began to pour water onto one another's shoulders. Wallmoden did not notice if they were pretty or not, but their silhouettes were very attractive.

One thing was certain: if these two girls were to be discovered in Wallmoden's room, he would become the talk of the regiment. He jumped up from the bed as quickly as he could and held the door closed, even as it was being pushed open from the other side. He heard Kaufmann's voice, who, as he was pushing the door, asked why Wallmoden didn't want to open up. It wasn't possible just now, answered Wallmoden. Kaufmann, who insisted on knowing why not, pushed even harder and tried to force the door with his body. Wallmoden felt for the key to lock the door, but as he could not find it, he let go somewhat and the door flew open. Kaufmann stood on the threshold.

He was carrying two large bottles of wine and two packs of cards under his arm. He looked at Wallmoden and shook his head, took two steps into the room and turned on the light.

Now, Wallmoden thought, Kaufmann will see everything,

certainly the screen, which he will no doubt push aside to find the girls. But Kaufmann's face displayed no intent along these lines, so Wallmoden turned around to look at the furnace. Incomprehensibly, everything – the girls and their dresses and shoes, the screen, the tub, the buckets and the candlelight – everything was gone.

At this moment, Wallmoden's dream was in peril of ending because he had the sense he had been dreaming. Nothing could follow except awakening. Perhaps he would continue to dream because there is the possibility – if only a small one – that the girls had taken their things and quickly disappeared while he had debated with Kaufmann. Or, perhaps he would not wake up because Kaufmann had said something.

He said: "Why did you hold the door closed? What are you doing in here that's so secret? Come on, we'll play some cards. I can't sleep. Not with these worries."

"What sort of worries?" asked Wallmoden as Kaufmann placed the wine bottles on the table and tossed down the cards, which flew apart. They were whist cards. He did not answer but returned to his room, also apparently to fetch Lieutenant Rex and Senior-Officer-Cadet Rosthorn from the next room, where they slept.

As soon as Wallmoden was alone, he went to the furnace. The wooden tub in which the girls had bathed was once again propped up behind the furnace, with the inside facing the wall. The screen stood folded next to it. Wallmoden had no time to inspect whether or not these objects had in fact been used. Even though he had found no trace of the two buckets or some candle wax drippings, he discovered something else which surprised him. He saw the wet traces of a pair of bare feet, which went from the place where the tub stood to the door leading into the hall. The traces were rather large, so that one might wonder if these were really the footprints of a woman or those of a man of small stature. The most amazing thing was that there were traces of only *one* person. How did the other one leave the room? Did she slip into her shoes or did she – unlikely as it seems – have the opportunity to dry her feet, or had the other girl carried her out? Is she perhaps still in the room?

Apparently not, since she wasn't behind the furnace where Wallmoden explored and she wasn't under the bed when Wallmoden knelt down to look. He did notice that Kaufmann was suddenly standing in the room again, this time in the company of Rosthorn and Lieutenant Rex. He hadn't heard them enter. He had the impression that his sense of perception would halt for a short while in regular intervals. It would skip a beat, would prance so to speak, and when he again perceived things, everything had, as if with a jolt, moved on. The three of them laughed as they saw him crawling on the floor. All took their places around the table, even Wallmoden who hated the game of whist, and there was pouring of wine, playing and smoking until his head hurt and the smoke hung like fog in his room. Still, Kaufmann did not want to go to bed. He kept refilling the glasses so that ultimately Wallmoden became completely drunk. He had the sensation that the table, with all those sitting around it, turned in a circle with frightening speed until Senior-Officer-Cadet Rosthorn stood and exclaimed in a thundering voice, "Ultra posse nemo tenetur!" Whereupon all ended in a general collapse.

8

Wallmoden awoke with a splitting headache. It was already day, but the dizziness had not subsided even in his sober condition. Even if he could walk without wavering, everything else around him was spinning. He looked immediately – for the second time, so to speak – behind the furnace. There, the inside of the tub did indeed lean against the wall. He inspected the insides, which were bone dry. It appeared that the tub had not been used for some days. Of course, there were also no wet footprints to be seen. He nevertheless had some trouble convincing himself that he had only been dreaming and he remained on the verge of blaming Kaufmann for the wild drinking bout for sometime thereafter.

His feelings of dizziness lasted until about eleven, at which time he went to the post office to await Cuba's phone call. He waited in vain until midday. Finally he considered that she had perhaps not yet returned to Vienna and was still in Baden, not having received his dispatch. He therefore sent a second telegram, this time to Baden. He urgently requested a telegraphed reply.

Actually he thought it unbelievable, or even more so, he would have found it unbelievable if she had not really returned to Vienna. He would have gone to Vienna, if the regiment had not been called up, and not have found her there. Should he have even bothered to look for her again in Baden? I think you overestimate these things, she would have probably told him again. And he would have replied: recently someone thought I overestimated death. Now you think I overestimate life. You overestimate both, she'd answer. They are the same.

After a while he discovered to his uneasiness that he was continuing the conversation that never took place. It was as if he continually heard her assertions and his answers. He tried to divert himself but always continued to be penetrated by these voices.

Following lunch, the two division doctors came to inoculate the squadron. The procedure took place in a garden, actually in the courtyard of a house that was filled with fruit trees. The instruments were sterilized in the kitchen. The soldiers entered without their shirts and took the serum in their chests.

When the inoculations were done, Wallmoden turned to the older – though lower-ranking – of the two doctors and pointed out his condition. The doctor listened to him for a few moments, while leaning against the table on which the instruments were laying in tubs of disinfectant solution. Afterwards he asked Wallmoden if he had previously suffered from the same disorders.

Yes, replied Wallmoden – yet the episodes were so unpredictable that he did not want to portray them as something serious. Currently, at least to a certain degree, there was only one incident, which occurred during a training exercise a few days ago – and he began to describe what had befallen him as the squadron was attacking the town of Wuermla. That is to say: he attempted to render a report, but realized after only a few words that this was quite difficult for him, or rather impossible. He would have liked to explain the essentials of the episode to the other man, but he was unable to. In order to express himself more clearly, he repeatedly described everything, but realized that he was merely repeating himself. His inability to render a proper report embarrassed him; he felt that pearls of sweat were forming on his brow and finally after several general murmured sentences, he kept silent.

The doctor had listened to him intently, finally simply looking at him. Now he said, "Don't you also find it strange that nature chose to utilize the principle of the circle, or rather circling or whirling in order to evoke dizziness and all that is associated with it?"

"No, I don't find that so strange" Wallmoden replied, as he was wiping his brow with a handkerchief from his pocket.

"Nature could also have chosen the feeling of falling more or less straight down, or the perception of flying, as in certain dreams" the doctor said. "Haven't you ever dreamt you were falling from a high tower? Your feelings may have been extraordinary, but you will have to admit that the actual feeling of dizziness, even a relatively mild one, is incomparably more sensational than that of flying or falling. The strongest sensations are evoked by nature through the feeling of spinning. Even when we get dizzy, for example at the edge a cliff, the feeling eventually changes from being pulled downward to the impression of standing in the center of a whirlwind. Man is never so beside himself as when he is turning, whether he is really dizzy or is getting drunk, or is deliberately seeking this state when dancing by merely turning in a circle or turning around himself *and* in a bigger circle. Dizziness has the same high rank among impressions as the existence of the wheel in mechanics."

"Well, all right" Wallmoden said, " but what are you getting at?"

"The circle," the doctor replied, "is the most perfect figure and the feeling of circling is the most perfect feeling."

"That may be," Wallmoden said. "You can especially perceive it as perfection if you don't feel dizzy."

"Oh God," the doctor said, "there are also people, for

example, the so-called addicts, that enjoy getting dizzy – not to mention that, in general, one places a certain value upon that kind of condition. For example, one can assume that the first religious acts of people were dances and one only danced for the purpose of reaching ecstasy. Long before every concrete idea of certain gods or higher beings, long before the appearance of Baal or Jupiter or Yahweh, the general tendency must have existed that a deity has to be produced out of one's self. Because to search for it outside of one's own person is always only a sign of weakness. Ideally one produces it out of one's self."

"Do you think so?" Wallmoden said.

"Certainly. And one reaches it through dancing, by putting one's self into a type of ecstasy, in which one feels transformed into a higher being, but certainly is more susceptible to the demonic, so that one also could have been able to perform magic or see ghosts."

"Possibly," Wallmoden said, "But at the moment I don't care much about one or the other. I feel quite badly; yes, almost ill."

"I rather doubt, though, that you are. You probably are merely in a heightened state of mind."

"I don't see the difference."

"Illness," the doctor said, "reduces the human condition; exaltation – as the name already indicates – raises it. But I don't understand why one must cure it at any cost. Why should one, when a person is finally a bit different from everyone else, convince him not to be?"

"I still don't quite understand you."

"One would also have to 'cure' an artist of his ability to produce artwork, or a tightrope walker of his talent to dance on a rope."

"I, however, am neither a tightrope dancer nor an artist," Wallmoden said, "and I therefore ask you to prescribe a remedy which would make me feel better."

The doctor, however, admitted that he knew of none. "Similar conditions," he said, "are, if rather rare, not quite as unnatural as you think. They are also, at least in your case, not dangerous. But you would probably really get sick if I decided to liberate you from this. I can't rid you of your type of health – even though you may not like it – by treating you like a patient. So it would be best if you just left this all up to nature. It will take care of itself as, oh, so many other things. In short, there are no remedies for your condition, not to mention that in the end there are also none for real illnesses" – a statement that convinced Wallmoden that he was actually dealing with a good doctor.

The next day also went by without hearing from Cuba. In the afternoon, Sodoma appeared in order to visit the squadron and reported to Wallmoden as usual that he had appeared in person and not as a ghost. Wallmoden was about to confide in him and tell him that he had not heard from Cuba at all, but decided against it. In the evening he sent a telegraph to Oertel and Drska and asked them to give him news. The next day also went by without his receiving an answer. At noon the regiment received its orders to set out at seven o'clock that evening.

On this afternoon the two doctors appeared again in order to give more inoculations. The older doctor, perhaps feeling that he had slighted Wallmoden, started a lengthy conversation with him. However, he did not talk so much about Wallmoden's proneness to certain illnesses, but rather about other things – mainly about old cults. He really didn't seem to be taking Wallmoden's conditions seriously. He formulated a rather chaotic theory of religions in which one would dance for cult purposes, and he declared that there could only have been one initial religion among the nations of remote antiquity which have long since vanished and whose names we don't even know. This religion was certainly widespread and thus there must have been at the time, far more than today, a true internationalism. Certain traces of this original religion are to be found everywhere between Scandinavia and Africa, between Peru and Mongolia, either in the shape of dance sites on flat areas, designated by stone circles or labyrinth patterns, or in the form of artificial hills upon which one danced. After all, the belief in the nocturnal dances of naked witches, and even the pilgrimages on to the so-called Calvary Mountains were nothing more than traces of this original religion.

Wallmoden, however, was only half listening. He had other concerns. He finally left and returned to the castle in order to pack his things. At six o'clock the squadron was getting ready to march on. At six thirty they lined up on the road to Duernkrut, but ended up having to wait until eight o'clock. At dusk the sinking moon began to glow. Silver mist was spreading across the swamps of the marsh. A most disgusting type of insect started attacking the convoy and bit the people in their faces.

Around eight thirty they crossed the marshes on pontoon bridges. Then they traveled all night wrapped in darkness and dust. They went through villages where people stood in the streets and stared at the convoy like wild animals with shining eyes, while lovers escaped from the beams of headlights into the darkness; they went over hills in which the enormous dust clouds veiled the forest like fog; and finally they went down into a valley. At the break of day they rested in a Slovakian village. Things were eerily emerging from the dawn light. The road neared the mountains – the Carpathians – once again. Around eleven o'clock, about two hours past Sillein, deep within Slovakia, they set up quarters. That was not far from the Polish border.

Wallmoden and Rex tried to sleep in a farmhouse for a few hours, though they did not succeed due to the many flies there. Constantly convoys were roaring by the windows. The entire

Army seemed to be moving. Even behind the house in the grass, which was sullied by ducks and other fowl, Wallmoden could not find any peace as he spread out his blanket. In addition, it was horribly hot. Finally, in order to at least do something, he washed and shaved. A woman with unbelievably fat calves brought him water.

That evening, the orderly officer of that section appeared and brought the orders to continue the march. Kaufmann hinted that they might cross the Polish border that night. Live ammunition was distributed and at six o'clock the regiment headed out for another night's march.

They walked through a mountainous valley that became ever narrower. The ruins of fantastic buildings were to be seen on the ridgeline that accompanied the road by the light of the stars. Around one o'clock they were ordered to rest. Immediately the order was given to load live ammunition and to put the blinds on the headlights. In the night between August 25 and 26 they arrived in Podsamok, a village that lay beneath a castle.

Everything was completely silent. The troops slept atop the vehicles. At two o'clock they heard someone shouting the order up and down the convoy to unload and take off the blinds.

Until around four o'clock Wallmoden slept in a barn. The next morning they moved into quarters in the village of Sedliazka Dubowa.

9

It was a village with about a hundred houses. There were also quite a few restaurants – you could have called them "pubs." A river ran through the valley, the Orawa. The railroad ran along side the river. At that time trains still came to and from Poland. But shortly thereafter railroad traffic was interrupted.

At the top of one of the hills above the village were the ruins of a church. It was one of those remains from remote antiquity, one that sealed the heights of the entire region, marking them with their own seals, like signet rings. Whether they were built to protect the land from the Turks and against the Poles or for other reasons was not clear to Wallmoden. He often sat at the foot of the crumbled walls and looked down upon the valley, which at this point curved around the hills of ruins, up and down, as around foothills. The weather was partly cloudy and it rained occasionally. Afterwards the sun would come through again; the wind brushed over the grass, which had been grazed by the herds, and bees were buzzing. In the depths the road was winding and the sounds were penetrating upward: the rushing of the cars, people's voices and the barking of dogs.

Wallmoden bought eggs, chickens and Slovakian cigarettes in the village. Whatever wine there was, was soon consumed. Wallmoden bathed in the river once or twice. The river was cold, as if it had come from far away in the north, and it was very turbid; the water was muddy or rather sandy. Wallmoden thought of all the rivers he had already crossed over. They all ran along sadly, as if they had come from a great depth. Once, as Wallmoden was walking along the railroad he saw an express train drive by. It apparently came from Pest or Pressburg and was going to Cracow or Warsaw. It was pulling a diner and sleeping compartments. But it was going so quickly that Wallmoden could not clearly observe the people sitting inside. It was as if the faces of ghosts were flying by. It seemed to him as if the train had come from a different world and was going into a different world. Here, however, was not a world. Here was something like a twilight realm.

They were not far from Zakopane anymore. From the heights on which the church ruins lay one could see the Tatra Mountains. Once there were people who had come to this area to hunt for chamois and other animals. An uncle of Wallmoden's was among them, and after that he often spoke of glaciers. But it seemed to Wallmoden that those glaciers did not really exist here, but rather only where he had talked about them, in a different area. He had been here in the 1890s. It seemed so long ago and everything looked so deserted, as if they would never return. For him and his type of people, it seemed as if the entire country were gone.

Lieutenant Rex received orders on the 27th to return to Vienna in his vehicle in order to take care of some official matters – which he did not go into detail about – and to then report back to the regiment.

"Listen," Wallmoden said to Rex as he was preparing in his room for the trip, "I have a favor to ask of you."

"Go ahead," Rex prompted.

"I would be very grateful," Wallmoden said, "if you could deliver a message to a certain person who is in Vienna."

"Certainly," said Rex.

"It is for a Baroness Pistohlkors," Wallmoden said. "She lives in the Salesianergasse number so and so. I have tried unsuccessfully to call her from Jedenspeigen. And I would be grateful to you if you would look her up and offer her my greetings, if it would not take up too much of your time."

"Greetings," Rex said after a moment. "With pleasure. At least, I hope I will be able to."

"I hope so too," Wallmoden said. "The thing is: I was supposed to meet her on Monday. However, I was unable to because we had already moved out Sunday night. Now I don't know how long we will stay here, but I suspect not long..."

"Yes," said Rex, "I imagine so too."

"I presume that they will pull our division back soon."

"Really?" Rex said. "What makes you think that?"

"It would be pointless to have us stay here indefinitely."

After a moment Rex shrugged his shoulders.

"Perhaps you are right." he said.

"All in all I am supposed to serve for one month," Wallmoden said. "And because I came to the regiment on August 15, my time will be up on September 15. I think it's quite probable that we will be back long before then..."

"Back where?" Rex asked. "Back from where?"

"From here," Wallmoden said. "Should we not be back by then, I would return back alone on the September 15, right? And I would arrive in Vienna on the 16th and would like to ask you to go ahead and tell the Baroness now that I will be visiting her on the afternoon of the 16th."

Rex looked at him. "On the afternoon of the 16th?" he said. "The Baroness?"

"Exactly. Let's say: at five o'clock –or seventeen hundred, if that's what you prefer."

"On the 16th at seventeen hundred," Rex said. "All right. I can pass on the message." "You must understand me," Wallmoden said. "Perhaps you have already guessed it, but this woman means something to me. Therefore it would be quite unpleasant for me, understandably so I would think, if I were finally to come to Vienna and she were, for example not there. Make that clear to her, will you? Ask her explicitly to be expecting me."

"Certainly," Rex said. "I understand. However, I would ask you to not hold me responsible if I cannot reach the Baroness or if she is not there at just that day and time."

"That is why I am already asking you to notify her now. After all, three weeks are a wide enough margin. And should we return sooner, this entire arrangement would be superfluous anyway since I can get in touch with her earlier then in person."

"Certainly. But maybe she has the intention of traveling or some unpredictable events could arise... Apart from the fact that you don't even know if they will really let you depart on the 15th..."

"Listen here," Wallmoden said, "you seem to be like the man who receives invitations but always has an excuse. 'Tomorrow,' he said, 'I am already invited, the day after tomorrow I have a lot to do, after that I have to go on a trip' and so on. – 'And the next week?' the other asked. – 'That week', he replied, 'I won't be back yet.' – 'And two weeks later?' – 'Two weeks later I have to attend a funeral.'"

After that both laughed, and Rex promised to deliver the message, got into his car, and drove off.

Over the next days Wallmoden thought of him often and whether he would properly deliver the message as asked of him. The squadron stayed in Sedliazka Dubowa until the morning of the 29th. Then they started marching and set up quarters in Trstena.

This advance towards Trstena put Wallmoden in a contemplative mood. Trstena was only a few kilometers from the border, and now not only were the squadron and the regiment there, but practically the entire division in one crowded area.

They moved out of the garrison town at night. The march through Slovakia had been completed in two strenuous, rather exhausting night marches. However, they pulled in to Trstena in the bright morning: they paraded in. The regimental music was playing loudly and smashingly, the engines were noisy, and the valley was completely filled with the rising dust. The colonel reviewed the moving convoy.

That was, as mentioned, on the morning of August 29. These were among the two or three exceptionally critical days on which Europe's fate was to be decided. Here, however, even though they were in the midst of the deployment, they didn't notice it at all. One could interpret the things quite differently as well. At any rate, Wallmoden did. Every consideration is actually an instinctive one; therefore, it should be a completely correct one because there is no wrong instinct. The intellect, however, always interferes and interprets everything incorrectly. It almost always leads to wrong conclusions. It is not nearly as difficult to have a right hunch as to interpret it halfway correctly. There is nothing more pertinent and yet more modest than the human hunch, and nothing more demanding and defective than the intellect. For adding and subtracting it may be sufficient, but when put before a true challenge, it fails. Since the things that were happening here were contrary to the ideas Wallmoden had, he interpreted everything incorrectly. He didn't see – or didn't want to realize – that the course of fate – even his own – was already in progress.

Near Trstena, the Orawa valley opened up like a gate to a vast region that reached to Poland. On the right hand side beyond the wavy terrain the high Tatras dominated the area. The mountain was built up like a castle. It arose nakedly out of forests, which were at its feet. Its peaks were glistening with a rocky bleakness. To the north one could see forever. The weather was beautiful. It was actually quite hot; white clouds were dissolving into the blue sky as if women's scarves were being tossed into a sapphire ocean from a ship.

Wallmoden's squadron was in charge of securing the town. Halfway up the road that led to the border a security checkpoint with an anti-tank gun was set up. One thousand feet down the road a group of about twelve men was stationed with an anti-tank weapon. At this point the road led over a creek and through a pine forest. There was a meadow in front of the forest. A river crossed through this meadow, the Jelesna Woda. This river was the border. (However, just a year ago the border was much farther north. And just two or three decades ago this entire area was deepest inland.)

Farther to the west the Jelesna Woda flowed into the black Orawa or Arwa. Two listening posts were set up at the edge of the forest right next to the road, and at about one thousand feet to the right, two more. There was a bridge leading over the river. Beyond the bridge a wooded elevation blocked the view. A Polish customs house was there. Three hundred feet to the right, at the river, was a mill.

Here at the front everything seemed deserted; only in the customs house there was some movement. The road in front of the house had been torn up by the Poles and converted to a so-called tank trap. On this side, however, the road had been shielded by a large amount of pine brushwood. From the elevated listening post one could see the white church tower in the town of Tschysne.

On the first day Sergeant Gasparek and his people pulled duty on the listening posts. He reported that around the break of dawn his people had observed a deer. He also brought some crayfish that he had caught in the river, which trickled in front of the forest.

Rosthorn took over listening post duty the next afternoon and received the order from Kaufmann to also bring back some crayfish.

The following day Wallmoden and his troops relieved Rosthorn. While Wallmoden had his vehicles pull into a ditch off the side of the road, Rosthorn was showing him the positions of the listening posts. He disclosed right away, though, that he shouldn't count on a quiet crayfishing session. Actually there was a lot going on. Some commanding officer or other arrived every few moments to be led out to the edge of the forest to study the area beyond the river where there was nothing to see. At the beginning, Rosthorn had assumed that the commanding officers had appeared solely because *nothing* was going on. When at the end a general had shown up with his staff, he changed his mind. Obviously something was being prepared for.

What was it that was being prepared for? Wallmoden asked, while crossing the river from which Wallmoden, too, was told to bring back crayfish. And what was the reason for these preparations?

But Rosthorn did not answer him. He just shrugged his shoulders, stepped to the railing of the bridge, and looked into the water. Wallmoden stepped forward, now also leaning up against the railing and gazing into the water, and offered him a cigarette. The little stream was running through yellow sand that looked like silt and wound along for two or three feet. The water was not deep but it was a dark green emerald color. The sun was blazing over the stream. On the left was the edge of the forest. In front of the forest was a swampy strip of land padded with heather and crippled pines. In between there were also some bushes and birches. In the distance the Tatra arose above the land like the blowing of high trumpets in an ensemble of stringed and woodwind instruments.

"I don't think there are many crayfish here," Wallmoden said, after he had been looking in to the stream for quite some time. "At least I certainly do not see any."

"All the crayfish have probably been taken out of this water by now," Rosthorn said. "Haven't your people already caught something?"

"Yes," Rosthorn said. "But it hasn't been much."

"Where I live," Wallmoden said, "there are no crayfish at all anymore. Supposedly there were once many of them. But now they are extinct. They allegedly had an epidemic and the rest migrated. They say they traveled great distances over land but they only marched at night, just like us; during the day, however, they took cover somewhere. Old people claimed they knew the spots where the crayfish rested. At my uncle Ortenburg's, though, one could still fish for crayfish. You would roast a toad, tie it to a stick and put it into the water. Immediately the crayfish would appear in order to eat the toad and you could catch them with a net. At least that is how we used to catch them when we were children."

"Really?" Rosthorn said. "Where was this?"

"In Carinthia," Wallmoden said. "There are areas there that look very similar to this one here. I used to go fishing with a distant cousin the same age as I, and with an old gardener. We only used to go the stream at night with a lantern but we always enjoyed it so much. The gardener told us many stories. He told them to us all summer long. He must be long dead by now. My cousin is also dead. He died in the war. He had some complicated injury which finally killed him."

Rosthorn tossed his cigarette into the water, then he turned and continued walking, and Wallmoden followed. They were now walking along the row of trees, which had approached the street from both sides. In front, the reed growth was covering the view. The road was white and shiny. It somehow reminded Wallmoden of the streets back home. That is to say it reminded him of the streets as they used to be. They used to claim that they were so smooth that you could draw on them. But of course there was only occasionally a horse and carriage that drove on the road. Back then, they also said, you could leave a watch on the windowsill for weeks without its being stolen. Naturally, ground floor ones were meant. And as he was walking along Wallmoden could almost see the watch on the windowsill on which the sun was shining, and around the window grapevines were growing. The watch was made of silver, it was attached to a thick chain and on that chain hung a deer medallion. The silver of the watch, of the chain and of the medallion was highly polished from so much wear.

As they reached the reed growth they turned right, into the forest. The forest was thick; blueberry bushes covered the ground, and leafy bushes were growing wild between the pines. On the left the street was glistening. For days now no one had driven on this part of the street, but oddly enough Wallmoden imagined that someone could suddenly drive on it again. Yes, he even believed he heard voices from people who were sitting in an automobile.

But of course no vehicles drove on the street. After a while they came to a grassy meadow, which was somewhat swampy. It was as though the tall grass of the meadow was a fluid running between the trees, this is how the meadow seemed, and the forest surrounded it as if with small promontories of land. One could imagine that the large leafed bushes that were leaning over the grass could carry snowball-like blossoms in June. A bird started singing, became silent and flew off. Wallmoden suddenly experienced the desire to stand in the meadow for a while; there was something he felt he had to think about. He didn't know what it was, but he believed he would remember it in a few moments. There was something in the swaying of the branch from which the bird had flown. It was something in the air, which was strangely mild; it seemed as though something were blowing along. But he couldn't figure out what it was. Then

Rosthorn kept walking and crossed over the meadow. He stepped into the forest again. Behind him the bushes closed and for a moment Wallmoden was alone on the meadow. But then he too, had reached the forest and also stepped under the trees.

From there it was no longer far to the front edge of the forest. The depression through which the river ran was shining through the trunks like reflected gold.

The soldiers assigned as posts lay at the edge of the forest and watched the tollhouse, and the noncommissioned officer who was to position them watched the opposite slope through his binoculars.

One of the posts reported in a whisper that the people in the tollhouse now seemed busy moving furniture from one room into another – for reasons unknown. Maybe they were barricading the doors. And at one particular window a face would occasionally appear. It was a staring, reddish, rather large and round face.

Wallmoden could not make out the face clearly but he found it to be ghostly in a certain sense. It was, so to speak, of animalistic ghostliness. Wallmoden was reminded of one of the toads he had killed when he was fishing for crayfish and which, while being killed, would remain without motion, as if they were the ones in the right. And somehow they remained in the right even when they were dead. It was simply the broad sitting-there of a mass. Wallmoden looked over with his binoculars but still could see nothing. However – or maybe just because – he did not see anything, this vision did not leave him during the next few weeks. Poland seemed to be staring at him like that face he had not seen; it did nothing but stare. One did not know what was going on inside and what it was staring at, and if anything or anyone depended on it – so it seemed – it would have to burst.

Most of the other windows were covered, Wallmoden

imagined, with featherbeds. A few chickens were walking around the house. The soil from the unearthed tank trap was drying in the sun. A large felled pine was lying across it. "Pluet super eos laqueos:" Rosthorn said. "He will let snares rain down on them." The mill lay subdued and completely deserted about three hundred steps to the right of the river. The forest covered the slope.

That was almost all that could be seen. The unpleasant thing was that one could not ascertain whether the slope were occupied or not, and by how many troops it might be occupied. It had been observed for days now but one could not notice anything. One marching hour east of here they claimed to have heard Polish tanks rattling along at night. But the reports from the scouts all contradicted each other.

Wallmoden and Rosthorn were lying at the edge of the forest for about a quarter of an hour. During this entire time nothing moved, or almost nothing. Nor did Wallmoden notice the noise of the water.

Finally he arose again. Rosthorn got up as well, and they turned left and crossed the road. Wallmoden considered what would happen if they were to come under fire as they were crossing the street. But of course they did not come under fire. They stepped into the westerly part of the forest and began to walk under its edge along the border. The distance from the edge of the forest to the river was on average a hundred and fifty steps. Beyond the river everything remained calm. They did not see anyone. A mountain hovered over them from a great distance – the Babia Gora. It must have been five thousand feet high. It was said that Polish artillery observers were on this mountain.

After some time, the ground became swampy and both of them had to pull their boots out of the squeaking mud with every step. But they continued on their way until they had reached the end of the forest island.

There were no people here as well. The forest started again a few hundred steps farther. In the distant southwest one could make out the houses of the town of Ustien.

From beyond the river a path led back close to where the field guards were. The path came from the high forest, and there was a ford where it crossed the river.

This path was torn into the silt bed the same way as the riverbed out of which they had fished the crayfish. It seemed – even though there were no visible wheel marks – innumerable carriages had been forced through here. The tortuous image of the horses and oxen and of the grinding of the wheels in the sand gave the impression of something Asian. The path came almost directly from the north and led to the south. But it still seemed as though it actually had come from the east and led to the west.

To the left and right of the path the grass had been grazed, but no herds were to be seen. Junipers were here and there. Wallmoden and Rosthorn sat down in the shade of a juniper bush and put their feet in one of the ruts in the road. Their boots seemed to whistle when they moved their feet in them because of the wetness. It was very hot and the juniper was fragrant. The sky arched like a cupola of glowing mist.

After a while they began to follow the path to the south. Because it led too far to the right they again turned toward the island of forest from where they had come. They ended up between small pines and bushes and they had to jump over several water ditches that were full of water lilies. Finally they reached the forest again.

It was the southern patch of forest. They crossed it and then they continued to stride across the fields. In the distance they saw groups of farmers harvesting potatoes, and now clouds were to be seen at the horizon. The fields they were walking across consisted of long and narrow strips whose hills were arched like backs so that the water could run down them. As they were crossing them they had to constantly go up and down these backs, and that was very exhausting. The ground was dry and dusty. Here and there were still some dried up oats. Wallmoden thought that they had not been harvested here either.

However, they already saw from afar, that at the posts where formerly only a few people were cooking potatoes, there were now many vehicles. "Well, all right," Rosthorn said; and as they arrived they saw that commanders and their staff were swarming around the posts.

10

The commanders and their aides were standing in a group with opened charts. Wallmoden's colonel was just having a dispute with a major from the artillery. Herr von Kaufmann was standing next to the colonel. "What is happening?" Wallmoden whispered to him. Kaufmann replied that an attack was being planned, but it was not certain yet.

The colonel was talking about bombardment of the town of Tschysne with the artillery commander. Wallmoden's major asked the artillery commander how long it might take, and if it were necessary to lay the town in ruins. "In order to pulverize it," the commander literally answered "I need eight minutes..." The regiment will attack from both sides of the road, it was said, each accompanied on the right and left by another regiment. Wallmoden's major drew the lines of attack of each of the squadrons on the artillery commander's map.

In the meantime, the colonel, who was anything but enthusiastic about the operation, as was later determined, stood there and looked around. "Well?" he asked Wallmoden, "Have you fished for crayfish yet?"

"Not yet, Colonel", Wallmoden answered. Shortly thereafter, the Colonel expressed his wish to advance to the listening post. "Come with us!" he ordered Wallmoden.

The group started moving and marched single file in the road's ditches. On the way Wallmoden had Kaufmann explain to him what was happening. They were expecting an answer by six o'clock at night whether or not the division would really be able to attack. If the decision were made that they were to be ready, the regiments would have to leave Trstena and the neighboring towns in which they had set up quarters at eleven o'clock and would have to set up a formation along the border. By two o'clock in the morning they were to report that the formations were in place. However, the attack was still not to be executed then, but rather only upon explicit orders.

They had been walking, and Wallmoden passed over the stream with the crayfish for a second time and then into the forest. The forest was completely different now – obviously due to the many people that suddenly filled it. It stood silently there, like someone who did not want to say anything more. At the listening posts everyone sat down in order to watch the opposite hill. Nothing had changed here though. It was just like before and the sun was shining on the meadow and the hill.

The staff was watching the tollhouse through their binoculars; everything lay still. After some time they arose again and began their return trip. They returned in small groups that conferred among themselves through the forest and over the road.

At the field post everyone got back in their vehicles and drove off. Kaufmann promised to send a messenger after six o'clock with the news, whether or not the orders to head out had been issued, and Rosthorn also put on his helmet and drove back to Trstena with his convoy.

Wallmoden remained standing alone on the road, and it seemed as though as he stood there he was thinking of many things but actually he had no thoughts. It was only the memory of the movement of Rosthorn's putting on his helmet that had stuck in his mind. It was the last thing he had seen: a curiously definite movement. Later he almost thought that the helmet had a jewel. He remembered a line from Shakespeare: "...the *one* helmet, which once frightened the air of Agincourt..."

The clouds had risen above the horizon. The sun was gone. It was four thirty. Wallmoden had his tent erected next to the road. The tent stood on a mound in the field. Straw was placed inside the tent. Wallmoden rummaged through his belongings for a while and prepared a candle for the night; finally he tried to sleep. But immediately the straw began to move at one spot. A field mouse seemed to have intruded into the tent, probably from the bottom, through a path which mice build in the ground. Wallmoden kicked the spot from which the rustling came. It was quiet for a while, then the mouse moved again. The walls of the tent began to move back and forth. The wind had started blowing. The air hissed around the tent. It seemed "frightened," just as at Agincourt. Wallmoden looked out, that is to say he stretched his head out of the tent while lying on his back. The wind was chasing the clouds across the entire sky, only to tear them apart again. The dust was drifting; evening had come. The clouds were gray, the Tatras seemed to be dipped in violet ink.

The restless wind still kept the walls of the tent swaying. The tent was small. It was gray-green in color and looked like the inside of a mountain cleft. It was still warm in the tent, although outside it was considerably cooler due to the wind, and clouds were blowing in and away again.

A motorcycle sidecar brought the food. Then everything was silent for a while. Afterwards Wallmoden heard a motorcycle coming again and a voice that asked for him. It was Kaufmann's messenger. He stepped up to the tent and delivered the message: the order to be on alert had been issued.

The field posts were to remain in place until the squadron arrived. Wallmoden ordered the tent to be torn down and then went into the ditch where the vehicles were parked, and issued the order that the troops were to pack their gear.

The people began to pack and in the meantime it was dark. A

half moon stood in the sky amidst fleeting clouds and sent down violet colored, almost sickly light. The land all around glistened like black silver. In the distance the Tatras could only be assumed, a shadow at the edge of the world.

Wallmoden sat on his vehicle for a while, then he returned to the road and stood there, for a few moments. Afterwards he headed toward the forest. To reach the advance party he had to walk about ten minutes. First the road descended, then it was at an incline again. The wind had stopped blowing.

The group was to the right of the road in the ditch. The people were talking to each other or sleeping. Two posts were on guard duty. From here to the forest it was about another one hundred steps. Wallmoden continued walking slowly. The road lay dusty in the moonlight, and the edge of the forest already appeared like a wall. In front of that was the bridge leading over the river. But before the bridge a dark stripe crossed the road, which Wallmoden had not previously noticed.

That is to say: the stripe or the band stretched out slightly crookedly across it. What exactly it was, could not be readily ascertained. It seemed to be moving, and although it was black-like in color, it shone a bit here and there.

Wallmoden halted. Everything was completely calm again, only high up the wind was still chasing the clouds. But in this silence Wallmoden heard a noise that was so soft that he needed a few moments in order to convince himself that he really heard it.

Or rather: it was not so much soft as it was unclear; it seemed to be comprised of a multitude of tiny sounds. It was a continuous, barely perceivable grinding, whetting and scraping. It originated from the band that lay across the road.

Wallmoden took a few steps toward the band, stopped, then started walking toward it again and discovered that the band was indeed moving. But only as he was standing right before it did he see what it was.

The band was about two or three feet in width and was not only moving across the street by coming out of the right ditch and moving into the left one, but it was also moving on the inside. It was continuously rising and falling a bit, rustling and scraping. At times it even seemed as though it were rattling with a slight metallic sound. It was crawling across as though a bunch or strip of chains that were lying next to each other were being pulled across the street. But the chains were not comprised of links but rather of animals crawling along. They were comprised of crayfish. The crayfish were migrating.

It would have been easy to laugh at this sight or to call the troops over and to catch as many crayfish as possible or to do both. But Wallmoden did neither the one nor the other: he was startled. He was mainly startled because he immediately remembered (and perhaps he had begun to remember even before he was able to conclude with certainty that which was crawling before him) – he was startled because he realized how he had leaned across the bridge's railing and spoken of the possibility of crayfish migrating. And it even seemed – as ridiculous as he might have thought it to be – that he had caused this migration. It was utterly foolish to believe that the crayfish that had witnessed the conversation, those that had been sitting in the creek, had been given the idea that they could migrate. But he was not able to reject the feeling that there was some type of connection. Perhaps it was the exact opposite: he had only had the conversation because the crayfish were already determined to migrate. He was startled to think that he was in such a state to have really felt this. And he was startled that they were migrating at all.

He could not have said why. Mainly he had not believed in their ability to migrate. Now, however, he saw it with his own eyes. But he did not understand to what purpose they were walking across the land. They were moving westwards in the direction of the Black Arwa. He would have understood if crayfish had migrated across land in order to get from one river area to another – for instance, across a watershed. These crayfish here before him did not want – or so it seemed – to go into a river area. It would have been much easier for them to keep swimming down their river until they reached the point where it flows in to the Jelesna Woda. Because it really did flow in to the Jelesna Woda, that is to say: it seeped into the swampland at the border where Wallmoden and Rosthorn had been that afternoon. The crayfish could have easily crossed the swampland to the river and then continued their way effortlessly to the Black Arwa through the water.

Since it was unclear why they did not even swim in the water, but instead marched across land – why were they marching at all? To what purpose, if they were not soldiers, did they endure the discomfort of the nightly march, which appeared to upset them already? They were progressing only very slowly. Wallmoden remembered that as a child he had owned a certain toy, a wind-up bear that while moving step-by-step would move its snout from left to right. Before every step it sounded a preparatory and strained purring which erupted from the bear's clockwork until it finally, quite hesitantly took the step, and in between rang the short, dry snapping sound of the mouth moving back and forth. In a very similar way the crayfish were moving on.

It is commonly believed that crayfish only walk the so-called crab-walk, and therefore only move backwards. However, a crayfish only rarely moves backwards. Normally it will only move forward, even if it does so slowly. By comparison it can swim backwards quite rapidly by beating its tail fin forwards. The crayfish were not crawling across the road much faster than snails, lifting their heavy claws, and moving their apparatus of many legs with great difficulty. With every step they raised their bodies, lowering themselves again after that, like icebreakers at work, and remained lying on the ground for a moment until the next step was taken. The scraping of the legs made a quiet but thousand fold noise and occasionally the bodies also scraped against each other. Indeed, individual crayfish had hooked their claws into the tails of the crayfish in front of them and let themselves be dragged to a certain degree. Wallmoden could not see how long the entire convoy was. There were thousands of crayfish! No one could have suspected that there were so many in the river! They came out of darkness from the field on the right and crawled into darkness on the field on the left. They were marching from east to west.

Among them were small ones and large ones, tiny and mighty, indeed gigantic ones of the type that one never saw nor caught. Apparently they stayed in parts of the river that were impossible to get to or in some underwater pathways of the rivers. The convoy moved on, scrapping and dragging, rattling and clanking like a squadron of armed warriors, a sum of innumerable movements, and it seemed unstoppable. It was as if it were one single animal that was crawling across the road, feelers touching, eyes staring, and armor shining in the moonlight. As Wallmoden was leaning over the crayfish and watching them, familiar words were going through his head. Even though it was he who was thinking them, it was as though Rosthorn were saying them to him:

...Et apertus est puteum abyssi, et exierunt in terram. Et data est eis potestas, sicut habent potestatem scorpiones terrae. Et similitudines eorum, similes equis paratis in proelium: et super capita eorum tamquam coronae similes auro: et facies eorum tamquam facies hominum: et dentes eorum, sicut dentes leonum erant: et habebant loricas sicut loricas ferreas, et vox alarum eorum sicut vox curruum equorum multorum currentium in bellum: et habebant caudas similes scorpionum, et aculei erant in caudis eorum. Et ita vidi equos in visione: et qui sedebant super eos, habebant loricas igneas, et hyancinthinas, et sulphureas, et capita equorum erant tamquam capita leonum: et de ore eorum procedit ignis, et fumus, et sulphur. Et ab his tribus plagis occisa est tertia pars hominum de igne, et de fumo, et sulphure, quae procedebant de ore ipsorum. Potestas enim equorum in ore eorum est, et in caudis eorum. Nam caudae eorum similes serpentibus, habentes capita: et in his nocent.

From the south the rattling of an approaching motorcycle had been audible for some time now and was coming closer. The motorcycle stopped at the field post, then began moving again and stopped for the second time at the advance party. Because it was driving without lights, Wallmoden could not see it. However, when it stopped he noticed it due to the irregularity of the backfires. The driver was apparently inquiring about Wallmoden's location and now began driving again.

Wallmoden was engulfed by the idea that the driver might overlook him as he approached, not stop in time, and run over the crayfish. Perhaps it was not so much the crayfish that concerned him, but rather that the driver should not see them. Why he, Wallmoden, did not want anyone else to see them, he could not say. He also did not have time to think about that anymore. The driver was coming closer and at a high speed. Apparently it was assumed that Wallmoden was much farther up front. Wallmoden ran towards him, to the middle of the road and started waving his arms to stop him. The driver stopped, dragging his feet and with screeching brakes.

It was once again one of Kaufmann's messengers. "Orders from the boss," he said, "Lieutenant, Sir, you are to withdraw the field post at midnight and wait with the convoy at the road for the squadron. The vehicles are to stand there."

Wallmoden was already in the process of replying, but suddenly found it to be superfluous. It seemed to him that above all he did not want to let the other one hear his voice. So he placed two fingers on the peak of his cap.

The messenger waited for another moment, then he pushed the bike in a semicircle, started it up again and drove off. Wallmoden gazed after him. He saw the moonlight glistening off the helmet. The messenger disappeared in the dust and smoke of the moonlit night.

After some time Wallmoden turned around again. The crayfish were not there anymore. Initially Wallmoden thought that they had crawled across the road some distance away. He no longer knew exactly how far he had run towards the messenger. But also after he had walked back along the road for quite a bit, he could not find the crayfish. They were gone.

It seemed very improbable to him that they could have disappeared so quickly from the road. The convoy was obviously not close to completion. Many were still following. But now they had vanished. Perhaps, Wallmoden thought, they had heard the rattling of the motorcycle and had interrupted their convoy. He wanted to search the fields on the left and right of the road, but he no longer knew the locations. He also found no tracks, the stripes of the light imprints they leave behind. The convoy did not start again either. Obviously there was not a single crayfish to be found here. Wallmoden was not certain whether or not he had been dreaming. He stood on the road for a while longer and considered if he should continue on to the listening posts or should go back. At the end he decided to return. Perhaps he only did so because he was not completely certain that the convoy might not again begin behind him. He, Wallmoden, would then have been, as it were, cut off.

So he walked back on the road and after some time turned left in order to reach the vehicles. When he had reached them, he began to inspect the troops' bags, but he was thinking of something completely different. Finally he said that they could sleep until eleven-thirty. He got into one of the vehicles to sleep himself, but he just pondered. The moon was shining into the vehicle, then it set to the west in the clouds. It was completely silent. Around nine thirty, however, the sound of engines came closer on the road. The vehicles were not dimmed, yet you could not see them. But they continued to make noise and the noise did not stop subsequently. You could hear convoys driving off the road and into the ditches. Apparently they were the artillery getting in to position, or tanks or some other type of vehicles. The entire area was filled with a constantly rising noise. It traveled from south to north, and vehicles gathered in all of the ditches. The land, even though you could not see anything, was filled with vehicles and people. The air roared.

After lying in the vehicle for a while, Wallmoden got up. The troops had also prepared before they were required to do so. For about half an hour they stood there, checking this and that. Then Wallmoden led them to the road.

The night had gotten much warmer. It was now heavily humid. On the road, vehicles continued to pull up. An enormous amount of equipment covered in tarps passed by: pontoons, munitions and spare materials. The earth was shaking under the weight. The dust was blowing in the dark.

Around twelve-thirty the squadrons came. They were marching on foot, weighted down with weapons, spare barrels and munitions. Sodoma was marching in front of his people. "Now," he said as he saw Wallmoden standing, "although it is dark, we are not ghosts." Kaufmann and Rosthorn were coming in front of the Seventh. Wallmoden let his group step into the convoy.

Right after that everyone stopped moving and they threw themselves in to the ditches with all their equipment. After a quarter of an hour they moved on. They reached the approximate spot at which the crayfish had crossed the road. Of course now there was even less of a trace than before.

In the forest, which was filled with dull darkness, one soon lost the direction to the deployment area. The rows also started to disintegrate. The forest's meadow was still clearly visible against the sky. But after that, one only sought the direction in a group. In addition, they came into the swamp.

At the edge of the forest the squadrons were shoving each other back and forth. In the middle of the movement an order was given to start moving to the side. The Seventh was supposed to lie a few hundred steps to the right of the road. The forest turned into meadows here, with single groups of trees like islands. The meadow was swampy. Under a few individual trees there was higher ground where it was dry. This is where the soldiers congregated.

The formation was not over until around three o'clock. The troops had set down their equipment and sat on the ground. While sitting they leaned their backs up against the tree trunks. After a while most of them were sleeping.

At four o'clock it began to grow light. The torsos of the sleeping troops had slid down to the ground and their heads lay in their helmets as in bowls. It was soundless on the meadow and the opposing hill was emerging through the dusk. It was the morning of the first of September. It was the day that the deer went into rut.

It suddenly grew cold. It was also lighter. The mill lay approximately in front of the squadron. Wallmoden, shivering, was talking to Rosthorn about the possibilities for an attack. They were conferring in a whisper. Rosthorn thought it to be certain that they would attack. Wallmoden, however, said that the orders for that had not yet arrived.

Yet at four-thirty the messenger appeared, his steps splattering in the swamp. He had been sent to the detachment staff and he handed over the order to attack at four forty-five.

118

11

In the quarter of an hour that Wallmoden still had, he was at first not capable of thinking about anything, but then a myriad of thoughts ran though his head. He thought about the last war, but not as someone who is simply thinking of something, but rather like someone who had forgotten everything that had ever happened since then. He saw, very clearly, faces from that time, he heard the voices. It seemed to him as though his people from long ago were lying next to him. He saw the uniforms from back then, especially the faded fur collars, which were lighter than the other material. It was as though something transparent, scurrying, had jumped up next to him like ghostly rabbits. And only as he began to continue his thoughts from there on, did he remember what had happened since. He remembered his return from the war. It was suddenly as though it had been yesterday. He still clearly saw the roads through which he had driven and how they had looked. He saw himself stepping through the door of his apartment. He remembered how he had gone out for the first time again in civilian clothing. It was all completely different. There were many new things, every moment something else. He saw revolts, parties, train cars with broken windows, women with make-up. He saw automobiles, hungry people, streets decorated in red, auditoriums of large theaters, foreign lands, adventures. He saw business people, slums, the blue of the lakes and never-ending summer. He saw gambling rooms, long winter nights, streetcars and people whom he had loved. How long these twenty-one years had been, how endlessly long! It was as though it were all unraveling in slow motion like a blossom with innumerable leaves. He saw himself putting on that uniform again. He saw Cuba, he saw the room where he had last seen her, he saw himself getting in his vehicle...

To the left of the road he saw a herd of riflemen rushing to the front, gray as a shadow, as they were running through the silver green of the morning meadow. They were running noiselessly. It was as though they had been exchanged for a herd of game, only half of their bodies visible in the high grass. They were already at the bridge. The interlude was over. It was war again.

It was, according to Wallmoden's watch, not quite quarter to five. He was still accustomed to the preciseness of advances that had been prepared with a beat of drums. He waited to see if at any moment the advancing troops would be trapped in blankets of machine gun fire. But nothing of that sort happened. Now his squadron arose and started running across the meadow and towards the river with the rattling and rushing sounds of many weapons and equipment. Wallmoden ran as fast as he could, because he was certain that on every part of the opposing hill the crackling of fire would start immediately.

But not a single shot was fired. Wallmoden jumped into the riverbed, the water reaching to his ankles. The bottom of the river was covered with pebbles. He waded through the water, climbed up the other side of the bank, and ran under single pines, up the hill, which had been hidden for so long. As he reached the top he saw before him open farmland that still sloped a little. Everything was empty. He saw not a single soul.

Everything had happened so differently from what he had expected. The time had begun when everything should happen differently.

The squadron approached and above, at a great height, moving forward, he heard a gliding whistle. Above the mound of the field lying ahead, a blackish, round cloud appeared in the sky. Well, he thought, now the shrapnel clouds are black, although they used to be white or peach-blossom-colored. But they explained to him that shrapnel no longer existed. It was an alignment shot. They only had grenades now. And indeed, the cloud was shaped a little differently. It didn't have a thing anymore, that one could not see. Instead of the smoke like liquid spurting to the front, it now gushed to all sides from one point. The squadrons advanced across the farmland. As they reached the ridge they spotted the town of Tschysne on the other side of the depression. It lay stretched out at the edge of a ravine.

On the left hand the peak of the Babia Gora was veiled in smoke. It seemed to Wallmoden as though he were being shot at with long barreled weapons. In reality the fog of the airplanes covered him. It smoked like a volcano from many craters.

It was completely light now. Wallmoden saw a few grenades hit Tschysne. A house began to burn.

The regiment advanced across a large pasture. The sun broke through the clouds. The grass was now emerald green. The flames protruding from the burning house licked it with red-gold tongues. In front of the town ducks were roaming around in the grass, quacking quietly.

As they reached Tschysne they stopped for a while. After that they continued towards Piekielnik. The road was on the left. It filled with the vehicles that followed them. An uninterrupted whistling and rattling saturated the air. The dust flew in veils.

But after some time one could see that the convoy was interrupted. The bridge in front of the customs house had blown up after some of the vehicles had already passed over. The rest of the vehicles followed after the engineers had reconstructed the bridge.

Ahead, on the left, a fire had begun in the village of Jablonka. The smoke was drifting like fog. One could hear some small arms fire. It was later said that a few Poles were defending themselves there.

The sun disappeared and soon afterwards it began to rain. It was a fine rain, like mist. They headed towards a forest, across fields, which once again had the horrible quality of many rounded mounds. The oats stood high. They had not been harvested here either. A rabbit ran off.

In front of the forest was another swamp and the swamp and forest ground were covered in heather. It was quite difficult to get through the forest carrying the equipment. The air was humid and sticky. "If it continues to rain, the vehicles won't be able to advance," Wallmoden thought. It was familiar, from long ago. The ground could become a bottomless pit. After two hours they reached a hill. From here they could see the houses in Piekielnik. But it was still far off. "It will take a long time to comb through all of Poland in these disintegrated formations," Wallmoden thought. Finally it had stopped raining. The sun reappeared and it did not disappear again from the sky, except at night, until the entire campaign in Poland was over.

It was about eleven o'clock. It was hot. They descended the hill. First they went through a swamp again, then again across the arched backs of the hills. The land seemed infinite. The Tatras were glimmering on the right, already lying a bit behind them. Piekielnik still lay in the distance on the slope of a hill. It was two o'clock when they finally reached it.

Their own vehicles were already in the town. Wallmoden slept in a farmhouse for about two hours. He had had the windows covered so that he could have peace from the flies.

At four o'clock he arose, washed and shaved. Vehicles were still coming through the town. The white dust was rolling down off the street, and the meadows looked as though they were covered in flour.

Around six o'clock the regiment marched on, mounted. First they drove towards the east, then northeast. The dust was swelling up like fog. They crossed through several towns eerily covered in dust clouds. In the late dusk hours they reached a bridge that had been bombed. First they tried to turn around, then they drove back and forth along the road, and after that the engineers were ordered to rebuild the bridge. While they moved out into the open fields, the engineers drove on to the front.

They slept under the stars. At three-thirty in the morning the bridge was rebuilt and they continued on. They went through hilly areas that started to become more mountainous. At the break of dawn the regiment started to assemble in several towns, not far from Novy Targ.

These towns were very peculiar. The houses were built of dark, almost black wood, and covered with reed. They almost looked like hunting cabins up in the far north, but they stood quite close together. They were built upon the hills. Narrow, sandy paths wound in between the houses, and over them hung ash-tree leaves and the foliage from maple trees. Wallmoden was trying to purchase some cigarettes, which he had been advised were available, when the march continued. The paths led up and down hills. The enemy was nowhere to be seen. They did come across a recently built position that had a new row of barbed wire, but the position was deserted, and apparently it had never been occupied.

Around nine o'clock the troops halted at a narrow, gorge-like valley near Sieniawa, at the train tracks. But, of course, the train was no longer running. Tanks rolled to the front. Several shots were fired, but no one knew who shot them and who was being shot at. The squadrons dismounted and started searching the area in the same disorganized manner as they had the day before. But this time they had to go through a thick forest and up a steep hill. They could barely drag their equipment up the hills. As they reached the crest of the hills – it was the Jamne mountain – they heard the sound of battle. The division had encountered resistance. The entire valley on the opposite side was bubbling with fire.

The fire, however, seemed much less intense than Wallmoden was used to. The machine-gun fire burst briefly and rarely – the Polish ones slowly, ours rapidly. Occasionally one saw grenades hit the enemy's field fortifications, which spread in a single long line across the opposite hillside. Whitish smoke was blowing. A few houses were burning.

After the squadrons pushed each other back and forth in between the forests, the meadows and the clearings for a while, attempting to find good assault positions, they reached the edge of a forest from which the Polish positions were clearly visible across the depression of a valley. It turned out to be a poor spot for concealment and it had only a single row of wire in front of it – like a cattle fence. The Poles were going back and forth in their trenches. Half of their bodies were visible. Behind this position there was a wooden church under some trees. The name of this elevation was Rozowka. It was about fifteen hundred steps away.

One of our own machine guns fired at them. The Poles disappeared into the trenches. A Polish machine gun answered. The cone of fire hit the ground about ten steps in front of Wallmoden. He saw something shiny fly towards him from the place where the cone of fire had hit the ground. He saw it quite clearly; it shone like a beam of quicksilver. It hit him in his right hand through his glove. He felt it like a blow and for a moment he saw black before his eyes. He took off his glove and saw his wound was bleeding heavily. He had not been injured during the entire previous war, and now he was in battle for one and a half minutes and was already hit.

He let himself roll back from the edge of the forest. A few people gathered around and bandaged him. Apparently, as he could still move his fingers, the shot had not gone through his hand. They wiped away the blood that was running over his fingers. Rosthorn was also already there. "Quit fortiter emungit" he said, "elicit sanguinem." Wallmoden lay on his back. They had taken off his helmet, and he was staring up at the tops of the trees that were swaying quietly in front of the blue sky.

In the meantime, the Polish positions were still being shot upon, and the dust from the machine-gun trenches was rising over there. A heavy grenade launcher was now in position behind the squadron and the grenades started to hit the ground in the area of the enemy's trenches. The Poles no longer returned fire. After a while, the first wave of the squadron advanced. Wallmoden arose and followed with the second, although he was still staggering a little. Now the Polish fire would have to start up again vigorously, Wallmoden thought. But nothing started. The first wave reached the Polish trench and threw two or three hand grenades into one of the dugouts where a few people were still sitting, and then took them prisoner. They came out thoroughly disconcerted. The other ones had long since disappeared.

Wallmoden spent the night on his vehicle. He was in pain and running a fever, and he only slept a little or not at all. The moon was shining and a few dogs were howling. Now and then a shot was fired in the woods. In the distance the towns were burning. Wallmoden was dying of thirst and wanted to send someone to get him some water, but they said the water should not be consumed, as the wells were presumably poisoned.

The next morning the other vehicles followed the squadron, and they reached the point at which they had attacked. It was very hot. Dust was rising up in high clouds like storms and rained down upon the meadows. Around noon they were in

Rabka, a spa town, which had been deserted by the inhabitants and where everything was now in wild disorder. On the roads there were only a few beggars and several dogs. Among the beggars there were many invalids who jumped about on the ground like frogs. The rubbish was bulging out of the doors. The water pipes and the lights no longer worked. The bombers had destroyed the area. Throughout all of Poland there was no more light and no more tap water available.

The artillery was firing shots all day long. They sent their shells in a northeasterly direction. In the evening they continued their march towards Lubien. Civilians who had been shooting on the advancing troops were herded towards the convoy. They were being led to their executions. Most of them had wrapped rosaries around their hands and were praying. Wallmoden thought about how God would act toward them at this moment. Probably he would remain as unprovable as always.

They continued on hesitantly with constant delays, sometimes for only a few meters, then on again for greater distances. Some other regiment was now the lead element. The artillery advanced. It was night and the entire valley was burning. By the light of the fire you could read the Polish recruiting posters that hung everywhere. It was evident that Poland had not even mobilized yet...

The convoy often stopped for a long time at burning villages. It was completely quiet then. You could only hear the crackling of the fire. Wallmoden's vehicle stopped for a while in front of a brick house whose door had been broken open. The windows also stood open, the casements swaying in the night wind, further inflaming the fire. Wallmoden thought the house was a school, but as he dismounted from his vehicle and stepped inside, he saw that it must be some type of administrative building. The doors were all open. He passed through government offices, but at the end he reached rooms that appeared to be the apartment of an official. Everything was disorganized. A bookshelf had fallen over, and the books lay on the ground. Wallmoden picked up one of them.

It was like most of the other volumes, bound in red leather and pressed with the red lily, that peculiar symbol that originated from the trident of a god of the seas. Wallmoden was surprised. One could have thought that the whole thing was part of an estate library, perhaps even the remainder of the famous library, which the wife of King Stanislaus Lesczynski had brought from France. One could not determine how the books had got there. It was an Italian book that Wallmoden was holding in his hand and it opened up at a "Venetian Song," and he read it, he the sleepless one, by the glow of the fire that fell through the window:

Sleep: the waves are beating against the banks of the Riva degli Schiavoni, and the Dome of Santa Maria della Salute and the full moon stand above the city like two soap bubbles, of which one of them, above the church, is still forming, the other already having ascended to the sky.

Sleep: the night is pastel blue, the palaces are made of silver.

Sleep: in their gondolas, black like Charon's skiff, the loving couples floating out to the lagoons. Dressed in silver fabrics and rose red, the women are sitting in the black boats. The color combinations are so bold that it is only proper for the bold peoples of Venice. The necks and cheeks of the beauties are covered like nuns, and on their heads they are wearing triangular hats.

Sleep: be without worries. This is the night of fulfillments. The ocean and the city, the moon and the stars are there as they've always been, and will be forever more, because the world never blooms like in sleep. No waking person changes the world.

Sleep: in your dressing table of gilded wood lie the delicate apparel you used for ornamentation: silk ribbons, fans made of black lace and pieces of fractured and painted ivory; and in a cover made of gold, an oblong bottle of rose oil.

Sleep: you are more beautiful than your jewelry. Your clothes have slid off the chair that stands next to your bed. The candlelight is playing above you, a honey-colored smoke. Your hair is thick and like spun amber. Your mouth is like a young flower. Your skin is the color of mother-of-pearl, and stars stand beneath your eyelids.

Sleep: the moon still hasn't moved the width of a constellation since you were a girl. Since you have become a woman, the stars that stand above the halls of Palladios have not yet disappeared behind the domes of San Marco. But only since then has the world become the world.

12

On the evening of September 5, the regiment arrived in Neu-Sandez. Already some friendly Infantry soldiers were there. They had come from the south, from the Carpathians, and were now engaged in combat with the Poles who were defending Neu-Sandez.

The regiment remained in position behind the infantry. The squadrons got into position along the left and right sides of the roads. Night had fallen by now and rations were issued. The people were crowding like shadows along the field kitchen. Wallmoden sat on the steps of a house entrance, and due to his injured hand, eating dinner from his tin plate was quite an effort. The cook had prepared an odd mixture of tea, coffee and cocoa, which he drank from his canteen cup. Since the wells were believed poisoned, they had to continue using the leftover liquid in the kettles. They had to eat in darkness and because of this, they often spilled food and drink on their uniforms and would then find to be covered with spots the next day.

Suddenly Wallmoden thought he had seen Lieutenant Rex among the people stumbling by him in the dark. He called to the figure. It was indeed Rex, who came closer and they greeted one another.

"Well?" Wallmoden asked.

"Well?" Rex answered.

"Back again?" Wallmoden asked.

"Back again."

"Since when actually?" Wallmoden asked.

"Since about one hour ago. I heard you were wounded?" He stood like a shadow over Wallmoden and was talking into the darkness somewhere above him.

"Did you have a pleasant drive?" Wallmoden asked.

"Yes, fairly pleasant." Rex said.

"And how was it in Vienna?"

"It was quite bearable in Vienna. But now it is just as darkened as here, you know. And then I also went to where you had sent me..." Rex said.

"Oh," Wallmoden said. "at... in the Salesianergasse? Did you have time for that?"

"Certainly. And I conveyed your greetings."

"You did?" Wallmoden asked.

"Of course – and I received the instruction to return your greetings." He lit a cigarette and the fire flamed in front of his face. "Thank you," Wallmoden said. "Well, and...?"

Rex did not reply immediately, but rather leaned forward in the dark and checked to see where Wallmoden was sitting. It was at the entrance to one of the houses. The people who owned the house sat inside. They did not dare come outside on the road, even though the shooting had stopped at night.

Wallmoden moved a little to the side.

"Have a seat," he said. "And what did she say, the... the Baroness?"

Rex sat down on the steps next to Wallmoden. "First I called..." he said.

"Where did you call?" Wallmoden asked surprised.

"At Frau von Pistohlkors."

"You called?"

"Yes."

"How did you know the number?"

"The telephone number?"

"Of course."

"Oh," said Rex. "They told it to me."

"Who told you? Nobody told me."

"There was this woman," Rex said, "this woman – I forgot her name – and she gave it to me."

"What kind of woman?"

"One she lived with. It was like this: first I did not call at all, but rather I went there. But the Baroness was not home and the woman told me perhaps I should call. She might be home by then, the Baroness – and that's when she gave me the number. And then I called. The Baroness was home and I went there. And that was already the second time I had gone there."

"What did she actually look like?" Wallmoden asked.

"Good," Rex said.

"No," Wallmoden said. "I mean the woman. The other one."

"Oh, the other one?" Rex said. "She looked like this and like that." And he described her to Wallmoden. But Wallmoden was not capable of recalling exactly what she had looked like. But actually it could not have been any other person than that one.

"And the telephone number?" Wallmoden said.

"I beg your pardon?"

"What was the telephone number?"

"Wait a minute," Rex said. "I must have written it down somewhere." Then he began to look in his pockets. He pulled out different papers and illuminated them with his flashlight. Eventually Wallmoden also began to help with his flashlight; however, they could not find the number.

"It really does not matter," Wallmoden said finally. "Tell me instead what she said."

"Frau von Pistohlkors?"

"Yes."

"Well," Rex said, "first she asked how you were doing. I told her you were doing well."

"Did she not mention why she didn't reply to my telegrams?"

"To what telegrams?"

"The ones I sent her."

"I thought you had called her."

"No, I did not know the number. Had she not received the telegrams? Perhaps she did not even know we had deployed."

"She said nothing about that," Rex said. "We actually talked about other things right away. I did say that you were counting on being back soon – but at that time the whole world was already convinced that war would have to come..."

"So?" Wallmoden said. "When was that?"

"At the end of the month," Rex said. "On the thirtieth I think."

"Why did they already count on war on the thirtieth? Nobody counted on it here."

"Well then," Rex said. "But now it is here after all..."

"I am not entirely convinced of that either," Wallmoden said. "In what respect?"

"At least it can stop again at any time."

"The war?"

"Yes.

"You think?"

"Certainly. For days now the Poles have been walking just ahead of us. The communication lines are interrupted throughout the entire country, they say. The electric lines and the water no longer work. The planes dropped bombs over everything... In short, these are catastrophic conditions. How long can this take?"

"I don't know," Rex said. "But longer than you think, for sure. Longer than until September 16 *certainly*. The actual resistance must still be coming. Admittedly I told the Baroness that you would like her to expect you on the sixteenth. But, if I were you, I would not count on being able to make that date.

Well then, let us even assume that there would be an armistice by then: you do not truly believe that they would let you return home immediately."

"What did she actually say?" Wallmoden asked after a moment, "when you told her that?"

"When I told her what?"

"That I would ask her to expect me on that day."

"She said that she would expect you."

"That is what she said?"

"Yes."

"So you did not give her the impression that it will, in your opinion, not be possible for me to come?"

"No. But it is not impossible that she herself was of that opinion."

"Why? Did she say something?"

"She did not say anything, but she could have thought it. Perhaps she also simply thought it would not necessarily be on September 16 that you would return – perhaps she supposed that it would not be until sometime in October or even some time later."

"Did you have this impression?"

"Yes," said Rex. "But she is expecting you, in any case, for this tryst."

"For this – what?" Wallmoden asked, surprised.

"For this tryst. Or is that not what it is called?"

"Did she call it that herself?"

Rex became uncertain. "I can no longer exactly recall," he said. "I told her you wanted to visit her on that afternoon, and she said: yes. I do not remember which words she used. It could be that I am simply imagining the tryst, but she definitely said that she would be there."

It seemed as though he had read that word somewhere. Wallmoden remained silent for a while, and Rex also said nothing. Then Wallmoden asked: "And what did she actually look like?"

"Pretty," Rex said.

"How was she dressed?"

"Very neatly."

He seems to have forgotten, Wallmoden thought. He saw Cuba's head in front of the pink colored light of the lamp behind the folding screen. "Did she offer you a cup of tea?" he asked.

"Tea? No – I think: a glass of schnapps."

"A glass of schnapps?"

"Yes. Or even two."

"You are not a good reporter," Wallmoden said after a moment. "At any rate: I do thank you for taking the time to go there."

"Oh you are welcome," Rex said. "I was glad to."

"The actual date of my return is still to be determined," Wallmoden said, "we will still see."

"Exactly," Rex said. "And anyway: perhaps they will send you home early, due to your injury, right?" And he stood.

"Yes," Wallmoden said. "That is possible."

"Let us hope so," Rex said. And with that he shook his hand – the left one. Then he went to check on his troops.

The next morning the Poles were no longer in Neu-Sandez. They had left some dead bodies behind – their faces were a green-yellow like their uniforms – and large quantities of peculiarly crackled canteen bottles, which indicated a trail of their path.

The regiment pulled out over the Dunajez. It left the infantry behind and continued the advance towards Tarnow. The second detachment was in the lead. Around noon they encountered the first slightly serious resistance from the Poles.

That was near Wroblowize. Shortly beforehand they had gone through Zaklyzin, a deserted larger village. It seemed to be strangely behind bars: the windowpanes were all covered by diagonally crossed paper strips glued to them, in order to protect them from the air pressure of the planes' bombs.

In Wroblowize the convoy suddenly stopped. They heard single shots. The squadrons got out of the vehicles and prepared for an attack. The assault was aimed at a ridge. The battlefield ridge sealed off the valley.

An entire Polish infantry regiment occupying the battlefield ridge had entrenched itself – as they found out later. In fact, in 1915, there had already been battles fought here against the Russians who had control of the battlefield ridge. At that time an entire infantry division had attacked and the battles lasted, if not for weeks, at least for many days. On this sixth of September the conflict was supposed to be resolved in a *single* day.

For even at the beginning of the engagement they could see single swarms of Poles leaving their positions to retreat over the hills. Apparently they could not tolerate the artillery fire – even though it was not yet completely on target. For that reason it was impossible to blanket the fleeing soldiers with fire.

Wallmoden's squadron, which had the lead, began assaulting alone at first, but could not continue the assault after about two hours. They were at the edge of the forest covering the right half of the battlefield ridge, between fields and isolated standing farmhouses. The squadron was in houses and barns and was firing over into the forest. The Poles answered with a tremendous amount of stationary machine guns, from a distance of no more than one hundred paces. There were a few casualties. The Polish weapons riddled the houses and barns, and a pig ran out from one of the barns. It had been hit in the stomach and its intestines were hanging out. It did not cry, though, but rather just stood there stupidly in the barnyard and grunted, until Wallmoden issued the order to kill it.

Immediately after that, Wallmoden's troops, most of who

were in a barn, suddenly were under attack by machine guns, from very close by. The shots could not have come from more than fifty paces away. The shots resounded in the most horrible way, and wood chips from the barn started to fly. But they could not see the Poles at all. They hid themselves excellently. It also would have been incomprehensible that they had not already fired, if one did not consider the fact that they usually lay cowering in their foxholes with their heads low; and only when one of the officers walked by – who were, usually, excellent soldiers – did they fight, but then they would hide their heads again. The farmers, however, had even more right to behave the same way. They had crawled underneath the barns. There was a crawl space between the ground and the buildings standing on stone pillars. There they lay, their faces to the ground, and pretended to be dead, even when one tried to chase them out with a club. Apparently they feared they would be hanged for spying.

When the assault team stood still, Wallmoden returned over the open field, but now the entire battlefield was alive. A large number of machine guns – presumably around sixty, since that is how many were the norm within a Polish regiment – were firing, and the air was chirping with the shots of weapons. Moreover, Wallmoden almost got into the burst of fire of friendly tanks, which, covered by bushes, bombarded the battlefield. The day was unusually hot, and running across the fields was certainly not pleasurable. In addition, thanks to his wound, he could not move quite as freely as he wished. He did eventually reach the street and walked along the standing vehicles to the front until he reached the command post of the division commander, where he gave his report.

The staff was in the road ditch, and the artillery had just received orders. Two squadrons that lay somewhat behind were still in reserve. The Poles possessed two cannons with which they caused much damage. In exchange, the friendly artillery poured grenades down upon the battlefield. The ground was being stirred up continuously, and the dust rose and left in large clouds.

One could still see Poles fleeing across the hilltops, but others stood fast with artillery fire. Above all, they covered the battle headquarters continuously with their fire from single machine gun nests. They even succeeded in flanking the ditch. It was loathsome. It was about three o'clock in the afternoon. Until about five o'clock the artillery was looking for the machine gun nests, but naturally did not find them. That would have taken days. The Poles with their two cannons destroyed a few vehicles, and a grenade killed a noncommissioned officer of the anti-tank gunnery section.

At dusk, when everything was engulfed by dust and violet haze, the tanks undertook an artistic maneuver by pressing in on the Polish left wing, near the estate of Lubienka. At the same time, the artillery was firing as much as they could. The battlefield steamed from the clouds of smoke and earth. But the tanks did not succeed in reaching the Polish main positions, owing to the deep water ditches. However, the two reserve squadrons advanced towards the elevations, but were stopped after five hundred paces by heavy machine gun fire and were stuck in a potato field.

Soon thereafter it was nightfall. In the darkness the Poles pulled back. Around midnight, the squadrons reached the elevations. The next morning the Poles had disappeared. They had left their cannons behind.

Around the evening of the following day they reached Tarnow. The Seventh Squadron slept in the vicinity of the train station, which had been bombed by planes and severely damaged. The buildings lay cracked here and there, and all of the tracks had become unusable. A locomotive that had exploded was emitting a biting mist, a smoke like saltpeter. On the tracks were long rows of trains that had collided. The windowpanes in the entire neighborhood had flown out of their frames. Everywhere there was a great disorder, and a few corpses lay around.

From the supplies of the train station restaurant the squadron helped themselves to drinks, cigarettes, and candies. They had acquired, probably due to the severe stress, a real greediness for sweets. From all of the movement in the heat and the lack of sleep everyone had begun to lose a great deal of weight, even though they were eating constantly; their boot shafts were already rattling around their legs.

Wallmoden inspected the tracks along with the other officers that morning. "From here," he suddenly said, while standing still at a certain place, "from here I went to the field for the first time. We had spent several months garrisoned in the city. It was here, where we got into the train, here at this point. I was eighteen years old then, or a little more. There were four of us and we had a wagon with our horses with us. I still know the names of the people that bid us farewell. I remember their faces. I still know almost all of the words that they said. It seems to me as though it were yesterday. It wasn't that long ago. It must have been about twenty-three years."

13

A migration of close to a million swept through Poland. It swept from west to east. It was made up of armies, of the followed and the followers; the fleeing vehicle trains of rapidly following supply lines, and of train cars. They fled until they came upon destroyed bridges or track switches, which had been bombed by planes – so thousands of these train cars stood motionless along the tracks. The migration also consisted of the horse-drawn carts, whose horses were starving and dying, and of the innumerable vehicles of the following rattling convoys, of tanks, of riders, of pedestrians in uniforms and those in civilian clothing, who ran for weeks and distanced themselves ever more from the depots in which the uniforms and gear that they were supposed to have gotten, had long since been in the hands of the followers. There were disbanding regiments of Poles, there were deserters and looters, there were people whose boots were hurting them and those who had thrown away their boots and were walking on sore heels; beaten, injured and sick people from cities and towns, who had been forced on by the fleeing armies to the east and had been displaced overnight, all dirty, hungry, sleepless, the followers as well as the followed. Shortly trains were no longer driving through the entire land, no horse was being fed, no cow was being milked, and the screaming livestock was roaming about the smoking farmyards. No connections were left in place; the enemies' divisions were losing all contact with their armies, the regiments with their divisions. Eventually only individual groups were resisting the attacks. But they were always being beaten and chased after; they ended up in captivity, or they surrendered; and they were losing deserters by the dozens, by the hundreds, by the thousands. To the left and the right of the roads there were many weapons and munitions that had been thrown away, ordnance and vehicles that had been knocked over. Dead horses with bloated stomachs were contaminating the air. In the area around Rzeszow a dead elephant was even found in a ditch.

No windowpanes were intact, no man was shaven, no woman combed, and the legs of the livestock broke during their escape as if their bones were made of butter. Towns were going up in flames, as if spontaneously. There was no food left, no more cigarettes, and nothing to drink. Even the crackled canteen bottles were not to be found anywhere. The houses either stood empty or were overfilled with refugees. No regiment was receiving rations, and the prisoners were testifying that they had lived for days off of what they had begged from the farmers. But the farmers did not have anything themselves. All the ditches were full of rubbish; the entire land seemed as though it were decomposing alive. Out of one hundred soldiers not even ten were standing by the flags. It was the most unprecedented or at least most arduous collapse of all times. And above this chaos, the monuments of politicians and artists of times past stared with rigid expressions from the cities' streets and squares.

The entire world had left houses and residences; by the millions the entire nation was moving eastwards in turmoil, without luggage, without the necessary food, following vague orders or hopes. This went on through mid-September. Thereafter, the entire migration began to move westward in chaos, in front of the Russians, who in the meantime had also entered into the war. Everything and everyone came streaming back, halted and remained somewhere between the Bug and the

San rivers, stranded.

Here several Poles also committed acts of true bravery. There were some, especially officers, who offered resistance to the end. But they did not know that they had long since been lost. They had been without real news for weeks and thought that further up north their armies had long ago reached Berlin... They did not suspect anything concerning the advance of the Russians; they knew nothing. They thought they were victorious everywhere – yet two hours later they were captured. Some, however, chose death over captivity, and hundreds of the officers of the troops who were also running into the enemy in the east shot themselves.

The entire catastrophe occurred in smoldering heat. There were days that were hot as in July, yes, even hotter. It was as though the sun had erupted like a volcano and was devouring the earth with its fire. Not a drop of the rain that the Poles were so hoping for, fell, the rain that would have rendered the earth bottomless, so that the motorized convoys would have sunken into them. Instead of that there was nothing but dust. It was yellowish on the paths and bluish-white on the roads and of a sweet smell or even stench, especially at night. It was foot-deep, ankle-deep, knee-deep. As one walked across the San River – or actually as one was already approaching it – the dust was enormous. There were regions, such as towards Wolhynien, where there was an ocean of dust, like a liquid, that stood between rocky hills that were turning pale in the sun like a pile of bones. And where the rocks were violet, it seemed as though the very tendons were decomposing upon it. The dust was all-enshrouding; it lay on everything as if squirted with water, in thick layers upon the faces and uniforms; it pressed, as if sucked in by capillary action, into the tiniest parts everywhere. It filtered into watches, into the locks of the weapons, into the carburetors of the engines, so that the air filters had to be cleaned every few hours. The men had wrapped rags around the weapons and had tied cloths in front of their faces; their eyes were getting infected, and the entire world lay under a layer of dust like corpses. In the vehicles it was accumulating as if ocean waves had left it behind like sand. It rose in huge clouds, it reared itself like towers, it clustered like storms. These veils drifted over the entire land, into which it dissolved and from which it trickled down like rain. One could not eat anything without its grinding on the teeth, could touch nothing without reaching into dust. It was as though mankind should be reminded that he himself was merely dust, nothing but dust.

On the fourteenth the regiment reached Rubieszow, and early on the morning of the fifteenth the Second Detachment moved forward towards the Bug River. The road was paved. The sun stood behind veils.

On the way they took one prisoner. A small, very young soldier, whom they had found near an airplane. The airplane had no wings. It stood in the ditch like a dragonfly that had had its wings plucked. But it had never had any. It was a completely new airplane that had never been in use.

The little soldier was not, like most of the Poles, happy to have escaped the danger and to have ended in captivity. Quite the contrary: when he noticed that they were continuing, he revealed unrest and fear. He cried and mumbled unintelligible words. This behavior should have evoked contemplation.

They drove, as usual, without tank scout vehicles and without tanks, since the advance had become increasingly faster in pace and they did not expect any further serious resistance. The Sixth, Eighth and Fifth squadrons followed the Seventh, which was in the lead, in almost closed ranks.

After some time they saw the village of Uschilug, at the Bug

River, sitting atop a slope. It was a very large village. Right ahead of it the road turned sharply to the right and then led across a wooden bridge into the village.

The Seventh was already nearing the bridge when they suddenly stopped. They thought they had seen Polish soldiers in Uschilug. Immediately after that, a hail of shots erupted from all over the village.

Troops and officers jumped over the edge of the vehicles and into the ditches. Since the fire was of a great intensity, a crying hail of shots swept across the road, and also the Polish artillery was involved now. It was once again only a few field guns in strength, but it immediately shot up several vehicles and wounded and killed quite a few people.

But also the small arms fire did not stop, and even less when it was not answered. It was because they saw no targets. Not until they started responding, chancing it, did the Poles pull their heads in.

Yet by then a quarter or half an hour had passed, and the Seventh had all sorts of casualties to claim. However, when their own artillery came closer and covered Uschilug with their grenades, the small arms fire stopped almost completely.

They were located, as Wallmoden later found out, right across from a dismounted Uhlan regiment. It was decided that they would attack the town: two squadrons were to go ahead across the bridge. The Third however, should cross the river Bug (or rather "Lug" as it was called here) on rafts a bit upstream and flank the enemy.

A considerable part of the day was spent on this attack. As the Seventh crossed the bridge, Wallmoden expected to see it blow up with all the troops on it. He also assumed they would be shot down by the Polish machine guns. But neither did the bridge blow up nor were the casualties during this procedure great. The Poles had vacated these riverbanks; they were now shooting from farther left. This decision might have been influenced by the flanking assault of the Fifth Squadron. Even though they had crossed the river in rubber rafts and had received several shots, they had successfully arrived on the other side and were covering the Polish left wing. By doing so they captured one of the enemy guns, turned it on the enemy and shot up the rest of the munitions. During this entire time the small Polish soldier who had been captured and escorted by a rifleman as if by a guard, walked crying along the road. They now knew why he had been so uneasy.

The entire assault had been completed with as much bravery as luck. At any rate the Uhlans were still in the town, and their artillery fired back at times as well.

Wallmoden stayed, as almost always when they were in combat, in the battle headquarters of the section. On this day the headquarters was in a group of houses not far from a bend in the road. In the course of the day quite a few people appeared the regimental commander, the commanders of the engineers, of the artillery and the sister regiments with their adjuncts and staffs. They conferred, but the assault could not be brought forward now. From the south they could hear heavy gunfire as well. It came from the distance of several hours, from Wladimir Wolhynsk, where the first section of the regiment had attempted to infiltrate but had also come upon strong resistance.

When night came, a small section of Uhlans succeeded – though it was unclear how – in firing up a cavalry gun near the bend of the road. It was still on this side of the riverbank and it fired several shots at the vehicles that had pulled back in the meantime. Apparently the Uhlans had come from somewhere in the west. But they disappeared again soon. At any rate, they were gone when the sister regiment came to the bend of the road to reinforce the lines on the other side of the river.

Upon the height Uschilug was burning, and tremendous

clouds of illuminated smoke rolled along. Here and there they could hear small arms fire from inside the town. It was seething like in a pot and reminded one a bit of the noise of battle in the Great War, but it was much weaker. On both sides the idea was now only to shoot when targets were visible. Accordingly, there were far fewer casualties on both sides.

Wallmoden and his commander spent the night in the house where the battle headquarters had been. The house was made of wood and had several rooms. During the afternoon Wallmoden had seen two women enter the house (they apparently owned it) – an older and a younger woman, probably mother and daughter. The young one had an ugly face, but had nice legs. She appeared to be somewhat urban.

Wallmoden did not see them leave again. But at that time the commanders had been there and at the same time two grenades had hit close by, which could have accelerated the disappearance of the two women. At any rate they remained invisible from that time on. Wallmoden walked through several rooms of the house but found no one. Who could know where they were hiding? He ordered straw placed high in the entrance hall and he and his commander spent the night on the straw. Nothing stirred in the house; the women did not make a sound, or perhaps were not even there at all.

Around two o'clock in the morning they received the news that the squadrons might have to clear Uschilug again. At that time no one understood this action – since the town had just been taken with great effort. But this was simply the first step in giving up the strip of land between the Bug and San rivers. For in this night the Russians had begun to push into Poland from the east. But this was not known among the troops. And not until much later, in October, did they begin to advance again at some width along the Bug.

The commander, an excellent soldier, tried to obtain the order to immediately vacate the area so that the retreat could still be accomplished under the protection of darkness. The order was not supposed to come, though, until dawn. Perhaps it was due to the uncertainty of the Russians' decision at an earlier time.

In the meantime, Wallmoden had set out to inform the lines of the anticipated moves. He walked along the road and crossed over the wooden bridge. The fires lit his way. Not far from the bridge he found his squadron lying on the ridge of a high elevation which controlled the town like a redoubt or entrenchment. The Poles were still in the town. But at this time everything lay quiet; the troops had fallen asleep here and there from exhaustion.

Wallmoden, as the messenger, passed on the message to Kaufmann first; then he walked along the lines, found Rex lying by his platoon and lay down next to him. The news, since one did not understand it yet, did not have a pleasant effect. Rex spoke of the casualties already suffered. Thereafter they both kept silent. The fires were being extinguished; only the smoke was rolling along in the darkness, and in the east one could see a gleam of the reflection of the silver feet which the goddess had set at the edge of the world.

"This," Wallmoden said as he pointed to the gleaming reflection, "So this is the morning of the September 16."

Rex did not answer and Wallmoden added:

"I mean: it is the morning of the day for which you had arranged the meeting for me with Cuba Pistohlkors – or the tryst, as you called it. You were right. It is not possible for me to appear at this meeting. I am far from it, farther than ever, more than one thousand miles. For I believe this here is the most easterly point that anyone of us has ever reached."

Rex still remained silent. Finally he said: "Yes, but also if the war were over and you were back, I still do not believe you would really meet with Frau von Pistohlkors."

"Why not?" Wallmoden asked as he looked at him. "You assured me yourself that she was expecting me today."

"She still would not be expecting you." Rex said.

"What do you mean by that?"

"I did not tell you the truth." Rex said. "I did not want to tell it to you. But there is no sense in keeping it a secret in the long run. You would find out anyway. I didn't arrange anything with this Cuba Pistohlkors, neither a meeting nor any other type of tryst. It would not have been possible for me. I never saw her nor spoke to her. When I arrived there she was long dead."

14

"What are you saying?" Wallmoden shouted. "That is impossible!"

"Listen to me," Rex said. "Didn't you notice one or another thing in the story?"

"What should I have noticed?"

"You really did not notice anything?"

"No," Wallmoden stammered. "What is it I should have noticed?"

"You spoke to Herr von Baumgarten about this woman, isn't that right?"

"Certainly..."

"That means," Rex corrected himself, "Herr von Baumgarten said when he spoke to me that he had actually had the intention of speaking about something completely different with you..."

"About what else?"

Rex looked ahead into the dawn and lit a cigarette for himself.

"Speak up!" Wallmoden exclaimed.

"Didn't you have contact with a gentleman at that time, who lived on the...what was the name of that street?" asked Rex.

"Which gentleman? Which street?"

"You did drive repeatedly to Vienna. What was that street on that you...I do not mean the Salesianergasse..."

"The Stallburggasse?"

"No – someone else lived there."

"The Piaristengasse?"

"Yes. The names these streets in Vienna have! Did you not know a gentleman who lived on the Piaristengasse?"

"You mean Oertel?"

"That was his name I suppose. Your car was seen standing in front of his house, correct?"

"Certainly. Kaufmann was in Vienna that day as well, and..."

"No, he was not."

"What was he not?"

"Not in Vienna."

"But he told me so himself!"

"He still was not."

"But rather?"

"I beg your pardon?"

"But then who was it that had seen me?"

"It was someone else. But whoever it might have been: Herr von Baumgarten felt obliged to...well let us say to interrogate you..."

"No, it was not because of that, but rather he had an objection about Frau von Pistohlkors, I am not sure about what, but he..."

"He knew nothing about her."

"About whom did he know nothing?"

"About this Pistohlkors."

"Why should he not have known anything about her?"

"Because he just did not know anything. He did not even know her name, but learned it from you."

"From me?"

"Yes. Had you not mentioned this lady, he would have warned you about Oertel. But since you had mentioned her, he interrogated you. For he naturally presumed a certain connection."

"What kind of connection?"

"Well, any kind," Rex said. "And actually it finally turned out that she was his wife."

"Whose wife?"

"Oertel's wife."

"His..."

"Indeed. Admittedly they were divorced. But that did not become apparent until later. At first one had to be suspicious of you..."

"Why suspicious?"

"Because he was as well. That is, after all, why Baumgarten spoke to you."

"Because of that?"

"Yes."

"But he did not say a word to me!"

"Understandably. He did not know whether or not you would tell Frau von Pistohlkors..."

"Who," Wallmoden shouted, "considered Oertel suspicious? Why did anyone suspect him?"

"Oh please," Rex said, "do not scream like that! The Poles will think we're about to attack. You scream before every assault."

"Speak!" Wallmoden said.

"To put it briefly," Rex said, "Oertel was found to be suspect, and it was not proven unfounded."

"What was not unfounded?"

"In the presumptions that were made about him or rather in the certainties that one already possessed. That he was still not arrested was probably due to the fact that they also wanted to be sure of the people with whom he had contact. They were interested in one of his friends, a certain Drska..."

"In Drska?"

"Yes."

"Some of the people seemed odd to me too, some did not. For example there was this Prince Septinguerra, whose family was too well known that..."

"He apparently did not have anything to do with the others. He was merely a guest."

"We were all guests."

"Well yes, but individuals – like yourself – were merely there for decoration and had no idea what was happening."

"They played."

"Pro forma," Rex said. "Only pro forma. But some very strange beings frequented that place too, like a certain President So and So..."

"The President? He knew one of my cousins."

"That is possible," said Rex. "But without wanting to offend your cousin: those are no credentials. Since actually he was presumed long dead..."

"Who was presumed dead? The President?"

"Yes. He was some sort of big business dealer or banker in his time, who had reasons to appear to be dead, but continued living under a different name. Drska himself – even though he really was a Baron Drska – was supposedly a swindler by profession; and then there were several different women, who either had the profession of being women in a peculiar way or were connected to some other sort of deals..."

"How do you know all of this?" Wallmoden exclaimed.

"From Vienna," said Rex. "I do not quite understand all of the connections – as I was also not all that interested. I am after all a professional soldier, and it is not my duty to occupy myself with such things. But I did learn a lot when I made the attempt to pass on your message to Frau von Oertel – or Frau von Pistohlkors, if you prefer..."

There was silence. The fire of the blazing town was crackling. The troops had fallen asleep from exhaustion. They lay there as if dead. Finally Wallmoden asked: "And what was it these people really did?"

"Many things," said Rex. "These were beings from a

completely different world than ours, with completely different ideas of honor, if one can call it that, and different concepts...But why do you absolutely need to know all this now? By the way one still does not know for sure yet, because when the story came out, the war was about to start, and most of them were already gone..."

"Gone?"

"Yes. Drska, for example, and Oertel..."

"Even Oertel?"

For some reason – not because of his person, but because of the certainly with which he always claimed to be able to guess events, Wallmoden would have been surprised had Oertel not distanced himself from them.

"Indeed," said Rex. "Also Oertel. That Pistohlkors, however, was still there. Her name was, as I said, not that, maybe her name was not even Oertel. She had come from some other country. Oertel was a foreigner too, but it could be that she had taken a different name in the meantime, perhaps because she married again – I forgot the name..."

"Was her name not Kouba?"

"Yes, that was her name."

"I mean: her last name."

"No, that was her first name. I do not know the last name any longer. But it does not really matter. In short, as they wanted to arrest her, she committed a stupid act – or perhaps it was also smart of her, since nothing else could be done – she defended herself with a small silver Browning..."

She was that type of woman. The men were gone. Wallmoden did not know why she had stayed; he certainly could not presume it had happened only because she had expected him! But she had stayed, and it had always been her way to defend herself to the end...

"Most of this," Rex added, "I learned from the woman with

whom she lived. An odd woman by the way, I mean: the woman – of a peculiar complaisance so to speak. She might have assumed that I was very sad about the whole story she was telling me. She was fingering around at my shirt buttons the whole time she was talking. We call someone like that a lapel scratcher, if it is with someone in civilian clothing. At any rate she seemed very willing to console me in my despondency..."

He interrupted himself, because two or three shots had been fired, and immediately following that a wild noise began. It had already turned gray now, and in this twilight the Poles attacked. Uhlans, oddly enough on horses, came up between the houses, but dispersed immediately as they received fire; they made room for other swarms that were storming against the redoubt on foot. In the rattling fire, and especially under the impact of the artillery, which immediately sent their projectiles barely above the redoubt, the attack collapsed after a few minutes. The rest of the enemies seemed to have the intention of remaining pressed against the ground in front of the redoubt. They were chased away with hand grenades.

The town had caught fire again. Wallmoden didn't find Rex lying next to him; apparently he was checking on his people. Wallmoden arose and left the redoubt. He returned to the road via the bridge. He felt himself thinking of a plethora of things, but did not know what it was he was thinking about. He was surprised, for example, that the bridge had still not blown up – since this, after all, had to be the end of the bridge – but of course he wanted to think about something completely different. It was a complete whirl of ideas in his head, of which he could not grasp a single thought.

The order to clear Uschilug had arrived at the unit command in the meantime. The squadrons were to draw back approximately the distance of the shooting range of a field gun across the river and also on this side of the riverbank and to set up a new security perimeter. One of the squadrons of a neighboring regiment was to cover the squadron while it pulled back. They were to occupy the positions that were to be evacuated and stay there until seventeen hundred hours. At that time they were to cross the river as well, and the engineers would bomb the bridge.

The Commander stepped into his vehicle in order to find the new position and he took Wallmoden with him. They drove for about five minutes, halted and examined the terrain. They set up positions to the left and right of the road: on the left it was to run along a cart path over a flat hill, and on the right through lowland up to the river. Behind that, off at a certain distance, there was a second position that was to be occupied by a single squadron. The Commander gave Wallmoden the order to stay at the intersection of the cart path in order to wait for the squadron and to direct them. Then he got back into his vehicle and drove on.

Even though the disengagement from the Poles took place during the bright morning, there was no enemy action. The reason for that was a simple one: the Poles were also evacuating Uschilug. Without having noticed that the squadrons were also pulling back, they returned towards Wladimir Wolhynsk. Uschilug remained empty, safe for the one squadron that was holding the left posts.

It was around seven o'clock in the morning. Wallmoden stood on the street and gazed towards Uschilug. It lay there smoking in the distance. It was no longer droning of battle noises. It lay quietly, only the smoke moving along in clouds. The hill had drunk blood as once before, twenty-four years ago, like all of those other hills over which one had fought, like the castle hill Karthagos and Ilions and all of the cities that had been destroyed. The earth had become sated. It was satisfied from the blood it had absorbed. It was the blood of the people it had born. Because where it is not satiated with blood it does not want to bear any more.

Wallmoden stood there, vehicles rattling beside him. He did not pay attention to them, but he stared upon the smoke that was rising from the hill, and he seemed to be thinking of the dead lying there on the hill, and of the dead in general. For now was the time when the dead lay everywhere on the earth. Perhaps the time had already arrived, the time of harvest. Perhaps the harvest had come ahead of time.

A squadron approached from the distance, marching down the road. It came in front of the sun, the people moving slowly under the weight of the weapons. It could only be Sodoma's squadron, for Sodoma was two or three hundred paces in front. And he was walking alone. Wallmoden had not noticed him immediately, and when he saw him he was already very close. He had all his equipment; many straps crossed his chest as if he were a shackled man. Since he had become so thin, the webbing laced his shirt together and his helmet shaded an unshaven and equally gaunt face.

Certainly it was slightly curious, just the way he was approaching, but Wallmoden could neither account for the reason, nor did he have any interest in accounting for it. It was especially unpleasant for Wallmoden to see him alone, as it was to be presumed that the Cavalry Captain would stop, and Wallmoden was not in the mood to hear for the hundredth time that Sodoma was not a ghost. And in fact Sodoma did stop. But how should Wallmoden have anticipated that Sodoma was going to explain the opposite this time?

He did so with few words. He said, after having looked at him for a moment: "I did know, Count Wallmoden, that you would not notice it, even though you claimed you would notice immediately. Since I have bored you so many times with negative information, it is a satisfaction for me to be able to give you positive information. Today, however, you are mistaken, Count Wallmoden. What do you say to that? Now the time has really come when you are truly mistaken."

With that he was nodding and smiling in a dubious manner. There was already something like the hint of a grin. His teeth, a bit yellowish and oddly exposed, glimmered in the shadow that covered his face.

It was an effort for Wallmoden to gather his thoughts and to understand what was meant.

"Herr von Sodoma," he answered, "I believe that since yesterday there are too many who find themselves in the circumstance to which you are alluding to make this joke appropriate, which you are obviously alternating..."

While Wallmoden was still speaking, Sodoma's expression changed completely. Wallmoden had not believed a face could change that quickly. "What am I alluding to?" he shouted as Wallmoden fell silent. "What is inappropriate? Why are you even standing there like that, Lieutenant Wallmoden? What are you doing in my way?"

Wallmoden straightened up. "Cavalry Captain, Sir," he answered, likewise raising his voice, "I am standing here because I have orders to direct the squadrons. Here is the position that is to be occupied."

"Then do not stand around on the road!" Sodoma bellowed at him with an inexplicable vehemence. "Stand where the position is! Step away from here! Stand by the trees there!"

And he motioned with extended hand towards the hills where at a distance of about fifty paces a group of fruit trees stood in front of a house.

Wallmoden did not understand why he could not stay where he was and what he should actually do over there, but his glances followed for a moment, the direction of the extended hand. As he turned around again, Sodoma was gone.

That is to say: Wallmoden did not notice immediately that he was gone, but in contrast the squadron was near. The first people were already very close in front of him. In front of the people walked First Lieutenant Hertzberg.

Wallmoden later believed he remembered that Hertzberg had looked at him curiously. But perhaps his memory was deceiving him. Anyway Hertzberg said: "Cavalry Captain Sodoma is dead. He died around four thirty when the Poles attacked," and since Wallmoden could not utter a word, he added a few moments later: "Where is the position actually? The squadron is to go in the second line. Were you not to direct us?"

Wallmoden, still without finding an answer, lifted his arm in order to point behind him. By so doing he turned around. In the direction that he was looking and where Sodoma had stood, the road was completely empty.

Wallmoden stood there with an extended arm. Hertzberg greeted him after a moment and walked past him. The squadron followed him, dragging along slowly. Wallmoden let his arm sink, but remained completely motionless otherwise. At the end of the squadron two people were carrying a body on a stretcher. The body was covered by a ground sheet. Only boots peeked out. Oertel would have found them to be boots of good quality.

So, this was death. That is to say: this too was death. Death had an innumerable amount of variants but all were of the enormous violence of nature itself, which buried lambs under the fall of a rock, which covers the life of entire stars with mile high ice layers, and lets worlds go up in flames. From far away it still seemed bearable – almost like a barrage in the distance – but nearby it was like a crushing blow in the front of the brow. And no one need rejoice when he thought he had found evidence that there might be a kingdom come. The kingdom come was apparently just as horrid as this world.

At that moment Wallmoden heard the report of a strong explosion. At the same time air defense fire resounded. About one thousand paces farther, already behind the curve of the road, black smoke was rising up. Looking up, Wallmoden observed four airplanes flying along the direction of the road at some altitude. They came from the west, but were apparently Poles, for shortly thereafter a second heavy impact followed.

Immediately after that, two turned; the other two, however, stayed exactly over the road. A few of the people from the squadron began to run off to the side. Wallmoden also prepared to leave the road after having hesitated for a moment.

He ran towards the fruit trees. Optimi consiliarii mortui, he thought – the best advisers are the dead, as Rosthorn would have said. He had not yet reached the trees though, when the planes were already visible above him. A loud ever-increasing howling resounded from above. Right in front of Wallmoden a noncommissioned officer ran and jumped into a square, man-deep pit that had been laid out under the trees, possibly to store vegetables over the winter. But Wallmoden had no time to follow him. The planes dropped four bombs in all. One landed about eighty paces away, and a tower-high earth-fountain jumped up. The next two were misfires. The howling swelled into a tremendously loud and shrill noise. At the same time the earth all around Wallmoden turned up. He had time to think that Sodoma's advice had not been all that good, and then he lost consciousness.

15

Quite simply, he did not have the impression that he had lost consciousness; but before he regained consciousness, he dreamed for some time and the dream continued exactly where his consciousness had stopped. Perhaps something happened within him between the time of losing consciousness and the beginning of the dream. But what happened there took place within a realm from which we, even though we sometimes enter into it, have no possibility of bringing back information – as little as *from* a former life or *into* a next life. There is no complete unconsciousness, but rather when we become unconscious (as in death) we merely drift from one realm into the next. But these realms do not keep any envoys, and only now and then – very rarely – particles rip away from the other realms and are stranded with us like driftwood from unknown continents, at the coasts of our perceptions; or like lost birds now and then, isolated souls, angels that have lost their way or gods, fall.

But however that may be, when Wallmoden began to dream, it seemed to him as though the earth that had risen up was now falling down like a patter of rain made of chunks and lumps, as a fountain collapsing in on itself, drumming on the grass. The noncommissioned officer who had jumped into the pit and shook "the dirt" as he called it off himself said: "It is already over"; at the same time he stepped out of the pit. Wallmoden looked after the planes but was only able to make out one of them, one that was just returning east from a bit south of Uschilug.

The impact of the bomb was five paces from Wallmoden. It resembled the funnel crater of a heavy grenade but it was man-deep and had a circumference of fifteen or twenty paces. A bulge of earth surrounded the edge. The funnel was still steaming a little and a trace of smoke was still hovering in the air. One could see a misfire in the distance. It looked like a short, compact torpedo and was buried more than halfway in the ground.

The squadron that had dispersed loudly was gathering on the road again. Wallmoden was wondering where the stretcher that Sodoma lay on was – he could not see it anymore. For a while he looked there; in the meantime the people were gathering, and they were talking to each other in a stifled way. It was as though they were mumbling curses. But suddenly it seemed more important to him that he inspect the funnel more thoroughly than to continue keeping an eye out for the stretcher. For some reason he found that there was no reason for the people to be gathering on the road, that they should rather occupy themselves with the funnel. He wanted to shout it over to them, but did not – he himself didn't know why. Perhaps he was of the opinion that they would not have understood him anyway. He made a half-annoyed, half-dismissing gesture and stepped into the funnel.

The earth that he stepped on gave way and as he was sinking to his knees, he slid into the bottom of the funnel. Here he remained sitting on his heels.

He immediately had a certain feeling of security. He could not see beyond the edge of the funnel, or rather: it was convenient for him that he did not have to see beyond it. The embankment that surrounded him in the circle smelled like fresh earth. He perceived it as pleasant to view the earth from such close proximity. It consisted of many loose chunks, most not larger than children's fists. The earth was moist; the explosion of the bomb had occurred at a depth in which the earth had still been moist. It was also still warm. The warmth felt pleasant.

Among the chunks of earth were bits of explosives. He reached for one of them; it was a bent steel plate with jagged edges, and as he ran his gloved hand over its edge, it was like running one's tongue across one's teeth. He threw the piece away and reached for a second. For a moment he thought that if someone were to come along up top, they would surely find it odd to see him squatting in the earth. But this thought vanished again immediately.

As Wallmoden was reaching for the second piece of explosive that was a bit deeper in the ground than the first, his fingers ended up between the loose bits of earth. It was indeed unusually loose and lay so lightly and loosely as if it were not made of chunks of earth but rather of slag that had been completely burned out, or some other very light material; yes, for a moment he even thought the earth was made up of empty wasps' nests. Right under the surface there were hollow places, and he could move his fingers within them without a problem, and so he reached in with his whole hand. It was a curious feeling to reach into something so loose. The chunks of earth rustled like a very arid substance, and he moved it away, having forgotten the piece of explosive, and in no time he dug a small pit. The bottom of the pit consisted of the same loose material again, so that it always seemed to go deeper. The bottom was completely porous and he suddenly had the feeling that something from the hollow spots was blowing at him like a breath. Something had to be lying underneath this soil and breathing; he did not know what it could be, but felt it necessary to unearth it immediately. He began to work and he worked at once as fast as he could. He already seemed to get closer to the buried being – provided that it *was* some buried human and not something else that was completely buried or had at least for some time been living under the earth. He believed he had only to move a few more chunks in order to uncover the face of the creature, but suddenly the earth was peculiarly tough and difficult to lift, and he saw that it was mixed with spider webs, almost like the air that one imagines in the realm of the dead, and in this his hands were caught just as if in cords. He could no longer free his hands from within, although he pulled with all his strength at the bonds – and he awoke.

His left hand had gotten into the gauze bandages, which were wrapped around his right hand, and both of his hands had become entangled into the ball of bandages. He might have lain stretched out, but he had risen halfway upon pulling on the bandage. He had lain on a medic's stretcher. For a moment he believed that since he was lying on a stretcher like Sodoma, he must be dead. Then he realized that he was alive.

He was in an ambulance. The vehicle was under way, apparently on a good road. It could actually only be the paved road from Uschilug to Rubieszow that it was driving on. The vehicle contained four stretchers or beds. Wallmoden lay in the left lower bed. Naturally he could not see who was lying above him. But he could see that on the bottom bed lay a man who was missing both feet. The leg stumps were wrapped with blood-drenched rags. He did not stir; his face was very pointy, and apparently he was either unconscious or dead. On the upper bed lay a major casualty. He groaned. A noncommissioned officer from the medics whom Wallmoden did not know stood with his back to him in the center aisle of the vehicle and gave the injured an injection.

At first, Wallmoden thought he himself was injured as well, for he was covered with blood. He let himself sink back, lay there motionless and thought. He remembered the air attack and the bursting of the bomb, that is to say: both were real to him somehow, so he simply halted the dream that he had had since then.

But he felt no pain. Also when he moved nothing hurt. The only wound he could find on himself was the one on his hand. The bandage was torn from it. He looked at the wound. He saw it for the first time since he had incurred it. It was not a large wound and it was already almost healed.

After a while he noticed that a drop had fallen on him. It fell upon his chest. After that a second drop fell. He looked up and saw that it was blood that was dripping down on him from the bed above. The body of the wounded person who lay above him formed an image upon the screen of the stretcher and where the screen was pressed upon the hardest, was a spot from which the blood dripped. Actually the entire vehicle was spotted on the inside with blood. He sat up. "Hey!" he called to the noncommissioned officer.

The noncommissioned officer turned around; he had just finished giving the injection.

"What is actually going on here!" Wallmoden said.

"Lieutenant?" the noncommissioned officer said.

"What is going on here!" Wallmoden exclaimed. "How did I get here? Is something wrong with me? Obviously nothing is wrong with me!"

"Indeed," the noncommissioned officer said.

"What does that mean: indeed?"

"Nothing is wrong with you, Lieutenant. I examined you, Lieutenant. Sir, you only had this one injury."

With that he pointed to Wallmoden's hand, but noticed that the bandage was torn off. He looked at the wound for a moment, and then he reached into his leather bag, probably to take out a fresh bandage.

"Then why did you take me with you?" Wallmoden exclaimed.

"Sir, you were brought in here," the noncommissioned officer said. "You were unconscious. How do you feel, Lieutenant?"

Wallmoden shrugged his shoulders.

"Somebody probably thought you were injured, Sir."

It could only have been like that. He had been transported into the vehicle because of his wounded hand.

"It is dripping down on me." Wallmoden said.

"I was not able to put the man on top into a fresh bed by myself," the noncommissioned officer said.

Wallmoden sat up at the edge of the stretcher. His head hurt. He held it with both hands. The noncommissioned officer reached for the wounded hand, cut the dangling bandage off and began to re-bandage the hand. When the bandaging was done, Wallmoden said: "Have the vehicle stop."

The noncommissioned officer spoke with the driver through a kind of telephone and the vehicle stopped. Wallmoden began to search for his things, but could not find them.

"Where are my things?" he asked.

The noncommissioned officer answered that nothing had been handed to him. Apparently everything had been left behind, even the cap he wore instead of a helmet since his injury. Wallmoden mumbled something and arose. The noncommissioned officer helped him, then he opened the vehicle's door. But when Wallmoden had set his feet on the road after having pulled himself onto the edge of the vehicle he saw an area that was completely unknown to him.

"What is this?" he asked. "Where are we?"

The noncommissioned officer walked around the vehicle and spoke to the driver again. After that he came back and cited a place that Wallmoden did not know.

Wallmoden looked at his watch. It had stopped.

"What time is it?" he asked.

"Two o'clock," the noncommissioned officer said.

Wallmoden must have been unconscious for many hours.

"Why did you not bring me back?" he exclaimed.

"We could not do that," the noncommissioned officer said. "We had to move the injured on."

"Where are they supposed to go?"

"To Rubieszow. But nothing was there. We did not find anyone there. Everything was already empty. Now we want to go to Tischowze or Komarow."

"Which crew do you belong to?"

The noncommissioned officer named the number of some crew of the division. Wallmoden deduced that this must have been the second vehicle in which he had lain. He had not noticed that he had been in a different vehicle before and had then been transported over. He honestly did not understand how he could have lain there unconscious for so long.

The road on which he stood was paved but the area, flat and hilly, lay completely deserted. One could not see a village, not even farmers working the fields, because apparently all had fled. To dismount out here would not have made any sense. He truly had the impression that the division, with as good as no connection to the rear, had been unusually far ahead of its own troops.

After a few moments Wallmoden stepped back into the vehicle. "Drive on!" he ordered. The noncommissioned officer shut the door and the vehicle began to move again.

Sitting on the edge of the bed that he had lain in before, Wallmoden began to observe the man who lay across from him, the man whose feet were missing. In the meantime his face had turned completely waxen and the noncommissioned officer confirmed that he was dead. He had been dead for two hours. Of the other two, the one that lay above the dead man was indeed seriously injured, but the one from whose bed the blood was dripping onto Wallmoden was not as seriously injured, even though his entire body was bandaged. A barrage of splinters and small stones had hit him, but he lay still. He had also stopped bleeding. All three of them had been injured by one of the bombs the Poles had dropped behind the bend in the road.

The stretcher case began to moan again and received another injection, but the noncommissioned officer said that it was doubtful that he would make it. After some time Wallmoden noticed that he was tormented by hunger. The noncommissioned officer gave him a bar of chocolate and after Wallmoden had eaten a few bites his headache was not as bad. While he ate, he thought about whether or not he could have incurred some internal injuries, though he had no external ones. How else could he have remained unconscious for so long! The non-commissioned officer, whom he had asked, explained to him that those would have already made themselves noticeable in other ways. It was hard for Wallmoden to believe that he had not incurred any injuries, because the people who had dropped him off claimed that they had been informed by the stretcher-bearers of the regiment that he, Wallmoden, had been hurled up into the air to the height of a telegraph pole from the explosion; this, however, was doubtful.

Wallmoden found it curious that he had dreamed he had been in the earth while in reality he had been in the air. He listened to the noncommissioned officer, and asked him afterwards if there were any water. Not water, the noncommissioned officer said, but rather some tea. After a moment Wallmoden ordered him to try to wash out the spots in his uniform with the tea, and indeed the noncommissioned officer succeeded in removing some of the spots with the help of a sponge soaked in the tea. When he was done with his work Wallmoden had them stop again, switched seats and sat next to the driver.

In the meantime it was already three o'clock and they arrived in Tischowze. But there were only a field-bakery and a few workshops that were actually in the process of leaving. So they drove on to Komarow. But when they were not far from

Komarow, they found the road, which had been empty – or as good as empty – blocked with a multitude of vehicles; there were engineers and other crew who were going back. Everything was stuck; nobody was able to move on. In order to pass the crews, they turned onto a field-path. But the field-path led ever farther away from the road, and upon trying to turn back, they ended up on even more wretched field-paths, and eventually not far from a village that, according to the driver's map, was called Janowka, but could have just as easily have been something completely different. The vehicle, after having made a disgusting, jerking, crashing sound, stopped.

The driver crawled under the vehicle, and afterwards claimed that some of the heads of the screws that held together the differential casings had been torn off, since the vehicle was certainly not made for driving in such terrain. In any case it could not continue on like this. The noncommissioned officer admitted that he knew absolutely nothing about cars, and also Wallmoden had no interest in them, at least for such things as differentials and the like.

It was not much later than four o'clock now, but dark ghosts, traces of twilight, were already swimming in the evening-like air, for they were already so far east that the summer time did not correspond with the actual time. The sun actually rose earlier than it should but it also set earlier.

After conferring for a short while, it was decided that they should look for a team of horses that would tow the vehicle to Komarow, and Wallmoden and the noncommissioned officer started on their way to the village. The noncommissioned officer was in a hurry because of his injured comrades, so he was nervous and ran along in the sand. Wallmoden, however, stayed back and after some time turned in towards a few houses that looked like an estate and where, as he thought, it might be easier to come across a team of horses than with farmers.

The estate was not far away, but while walking, his body started to ache. Who really knew how high he had been thrown through the air? It was a miracle that he had not fractured anything. Even his teeth seemed peculiar in his mouth now. His right cheekbone hurt; perhaps he had fallen onto his face. In contrast, his head had stopped aching.

The estate was in a type of sand desert. Like most of the estates in this area it proved to be quite large. The farm buildings were a village all their own. But everything lay empty, save only a few cows which had to be milked and which were screaming and scurrying among the buildings.

But the people were gone; he saw no one. The residence stood under trees that belonged to a large garden. The garden had grown wild, and even the house looked neglected. The door was under a porch that carried a balcony. It stood open and the wind moved it in its hinges, squeaking softly. Wild wine vines grew up the wall.

This door that moved like the wings of a large, dying bird, reminded him of something but he could not say of what. He stepped onto the stone-paved forecourt that lay lower than the garden and then, after a moment, into the hall. There in the hall everything lay in disarray. Some troops – one pulling back or one following – might have stayed in the house. Also the doors that led into the rooms all stood open. For now the time had come when no one deemed it necessary to close doors any longer. A flight of stairs led to the upper level.

The house was plentifully furnished and the floors were carpeted. But nothing was in its place. The wind blew through the open doors and windows. It walked on silent feet, but it seemed as though it were crying as it went through the house. It was a completely unknown house through which the wind cried, but it seemed to Wallmoden as though he somehow knew it. A person thinks he knows all the houses in which other people had lived which are similar to one's own.

Wallmoden stood in the hallway. He could not have said what he was actually looking for. Actually, what he had really wanted to find was a team of horses, though there was none to be found here. Yet, instead of leaving again, he began to look around in the hallway, although he did not know why. Pictures hung on the walls, large darkened paintings, and after some time he saw that they represented the Alexander convoy – the people wore a type of traditional Turkish costume – and among them hung colored etchings, antlers, a frame with walking-sticks and horsewhips and a green wallpapered board on which silver-mounted boar tusks and deer antlers hung.

Wallmoden regarded everything with attention. It seemed to him long ago since he had had the opportunity to truly observe anything, and he began to delve into the sight of these things, imagining the strength of the game which had borne the antlers, and he inspected the sticks and horsewhips for their usability. None of this was his business, yet he even went through the broken slabs of the china cupboard and inspected the porcelain as if he were in the process of checking what had to be replaced at home.

But after that, as he also walked through the other rooms, he ended up in one – the last one – that was completely ugly in its disorderliness. The disorderliness suddenly repulsed him, and although he did not know in what context it might have happened, he remembered the death of Cuba in this room. The death of this woman, loss and destruction in general were of utter ugliness to him. He attempted to think of something else, quickly left the rooms and stepped into the hallway again. He was already in the process of leaving the house, but after a moment of hesitation he walked up the stairs.

There were also rugs on the stairs, but they were full of dust.

It was as though, due to some large tremor through the entire house, the whitewash had fallen from the ceilings and now lay as a layer on the carpets. He stepped into the upper hallway, and the carpets were also full of dust here, but after two or three steps he suddenly stood still.

In front of him in the dust that lay on the carpet he saw the wet tracks of two naked feet: in fact they came out of a door that was on his left and led to a door at the other end of the hallway.

The tracks were still very fresh. They showed up clearly and were literally surrounded by water, as if the person that had walked here had been dripping. Single water beads that had been covered by dust had, like little drops of quicksilver, rolled on over the carpet like little balls. There they still lay or had already dissolved, although it could not have been in all more than a minute ago when the footprints had developed. They were the footprints of a man of short stature – or of a tall woman.

Wallmoden stared at the footprints, and for a moment he felt himself simply thinking of how they had got there, but the next moment he knew that he had seen them before. Yes, he could have sworn he was seeing them again.

It was exactly the same type of footprint that he had seen in the dream in his room in Jedenspeigen Castle, that time when he sensed two women had come into his room but only one had left it. It certainly could not be that these were the footprints of the same feet. For how could the dreamed illusions have come here! But they were the continuation of those others that had at that time led somewhere and that now reappeared here from somewhere else.

It would not have made sense to ponder where those feet had stepped in the meantime, where the mysterious river, from which they were still wet, streamed. However, there is no doubt that we – and how often! – for moments, for days, yes even sometimes for longer periods of times, are in completely different realms, even when we think we are here, and we live a life there and do things of which we know nothing. But we do live it, this life, and perhaps it is the real one. And what befalls us also befalls others. Sometimes we disappear in those areas, sometimes things that cannot take place there take place here – and again we have to go through those shadowy rivers so that we can change. For there can be no return without any change.

The times of being absent seem infinite while they last, but in the moments of reunion, they are like nothing. Also for Wallmoden the time that had passed between the dream and the rediscovery of the footprints was as if it were not there. Why, he thought, did I not actually open the door of that hallway and follow the footprints? But I would not have come anywhere else but here. Now I am here, and it does not matter where I have been in the meantime – where we all have been in the meantime.

He followed the steps. Only a latch closed the door behind which they disappeared. He opened it and stepped into a small vestibule, a type of private vestibule. From here a second door led into a room. That door stood open. It could have been a bedroom. Through the door he saw a mirror between two windows. The mirror reached to the floor and in front of the mirror stood a woman.

It could only be that same one from whom the footprints originated. She was naked and her skin shone from wetness. She had her back turned to him, but he saw her in the mirror before him as if she were looking at him. A cascade of blond, almost yellow hair, that ran out in long strands, hung down her back, and she had taken her hair up in both hands and was wringing the water out of it.

She was a tall, young woman, and her figure glistened. It seemed in the blurring of the mirror as though she were floating a bit above the floor. The buds of her bosoms stared like the tips of lances dipped in rose-colored blood.

He did not know her, had never seen her. It was not one of the two maidservants from Jedenspeigen, the blonde, as she appeared in his dreams, she, who had a face as small as the black one, but rather they both were completely blurry in their expressions and had walked like sleepwalkers. It was also not one of those other women he knew. She was a complete stranger to him. She did not see him in the mirror; she looked upon the reflection of her hair from which she was wringing out the water, as though she were wringing it out of the reflection.

The strangest thing was that he, even though he looked straight at her, could not have said what she looked like; but rather it seemed to him that even though he saw her completely in reality and in the mirror, it was as if he did not see her but rather the perception of great beauty. Without a doubt the sense of beauty does not lie determined in the concreteness of an individual beautiful thing or person. Rather its purpose is much more the enchantment of the soul. There is nothing physical that is not made with the intent of affecting the soul, and there is no soul that does not intend to dazzle everything physical with its sensations.

It was as if every part of her body were shooting off gleaming arrows that either hit him in straight flight or were thrust back on him from the mirror like broken rays, every beam that emitted from her surface hitting him, like an arrow on whose feathers gold colored strings from her hair had become entangled, and beauty was transmitted to him. But the sum of the light loads carried by the arrows did not make up the total picture of this woman. It seemed to him as though instead of seeing her, he saw something completely different.

It was as though a great perspective in a gleaming width or distance was opening for him, and one could not immediately perceive what it contained. For it was a multitude of things that did not evoke feelings, but rather was first evoked by the feelings.

It seemed as though an ocean were waving around islands that swam between the blue of the sky and of the ocean, and on which there were all the things that ever intoxicate the soul: scents and valuable instruments, waterfalls that fall into enchanted canyons, the glory of lovely limbs, ghosts that glisten like blades, gods, rainbows and thrones made of gold and ivory. But the architecture of these things was far more complicated than that of a mere coexistence. They melted into each other with complete freedom. The foot of the palaces stood on swimming ships and the godly thought, so it seemed, nested in the smoking mouth of the volcanoes or in the jewelry of women.

It was not comprehensible to this motionless, staring person how in this shattered land, in which starving and dirty creatures sneak by houses, he still could have found a creature whose sight would generate all of this. It was apparently not the present that he saw; it was in some sense a face of the future. The future never becomes as clear, but it is also never closer than when it seems farther than ever.

What did this person have to do with the radiance that it evoked in the soul? Nothing. She did not even suspect this radiance. No woman suspects it. It was a completely unfamiliar woman whom he had surprised in front of a mirror. That was all. He had entered completely by chance. But none of us knows what kind of missions we actually carry out, what kind of things we actually do.

He stepped back soundlessly, left the vestibule and left the door on the latch again. He stood still for a moment in the hallway, and after that he turned and returned to the stairs. He had been full of tremendous anticipation since he had seen the footprints, and now, even if only for a moment, he smiled. Nothing more had happened than that he had surprised a woman, apparently after a bath. He walked down the stairs and through the downstairs hallway. Then he left the house.

To the point where he had left the vehicle he had about a ten-minute walk. But he already saw from afar that the vehicle was no longer standing there. Apparently it had already been towed and it would have been futile to look for it even in the village. The vehicle was certainly no longer in the village. It might already be on its way to Komarow.

He found it to be understandable that the noncommissioned officer did not wait for him. He had the wounded, and he, Wallmoden, was not even wounded. He might have been gone for an hour in all. He had wound up and reset his watch when he had asked the noncommissioned officer what time it was. Now it showed that it was a few minutes after five. It was twilight.

But he found it peculiar that he now stood in an empty field without luggage, without weapons and even without a cap, at the end of the whole story. An Uhlan patrol could still appear at the ridge of a hill, chase him down and stab him.

He turned around, put his hands in his pockets and returned to the house. He had a peculiar feeling, the impression that he had rid himself of everything extraneous and he was merely himself. Like that, with his hands in his pockets, even kings might have walked away from somewhere, and those might not have even been their worst moments.

While walking, his right inner heel began to ache. He stopped and moved his heel back and forth in the boot. Something was in his boot. Probably the leather lining had torn and it might have been worn through. So, he thought, now he had torn boots. That is appropriate for someone who had once been stabbed while on a horse and who afterwards had also lost all of his vehicles. Now the actual migration could begin. After all, he should have owned a second pair of boots by now. But he would not have profited from them. They would have lain on his truck, God only knows where. It was peculiar – it went through his mind – that he would have gained nothing from these boots after all.

When he came onto the estate, the livestock was still howling. The cows stared and howled into nothingness, trotted a few steps, stopped anew and began howling once more.

He stepped into the house, walked up the stairs and through the upstairs hallway. The footprints were still visible in the dust of the carpets, but the moisture was already soaked up, and one could only see the contours in the dust. He followed the footprints again and opened the door that he had already opened once, a second time.

The young woman now sat on the bed with her face lowered. She had wrapped her hair in a cloth. When she heard the door open, she raised her head and simultaneously closed the robe that was hanging around her shoulders.

Wallmoden stepped to the second door and remained standing there. He thought she might be startled, but she just looked up, unperturbed. She had brown eyes, which made an odd contrast to her hair. One did not see the hair, but its reflection lived in the color of her skin.

"Excuse me for intruding," he said in French. "But the circumstances might excuse my behavior. Could you tell me what place this is and where I actually am?"

16

She did not answer him, but merely stared at him and as she sat on the bed she pulled her feet under the dressing gown. Since he presumed that she had not understood him, he repeated what he had already said once in English.

"I do not know," she replied in German. "I am afraid I do not know any more than you."

"Are you not from here?" he asked. "Are you not Polish?"

Again she only replied after a moment. "No," she said. "But where are you from? Why do you also not know where you are?"

"My people," he said, "claimed this is Janowka. But they are gone, and actually they were not even my people."

"Why were they not your people?"

"They just took me along," he said. "We came from Tischowze and wanted to go to Komarow. How far is it still to Komarow?"

She shrugged her shoulders. "How should I know?" she said. "I do not even know that it exists. I do not know anything."

"What are you trying to say by that?"

"I was brought to somewhere in this area," she said. "But this afternoon they all were gone and I walked here after a while because I thought there would have to be people here. Nobody was in the house but I could not have made myself understood to anyone anyway – perhaps in English, but not even the people who had owned the house were here any longer."

"From where did they actually bring you?"

"From Cracow."

"From Cracow?"

"Yes. When the war first started they moved us all away, first with trains, but they only went to Dembiza, then they brought me further with a vehicle, and finally I had to go by foot. All that took until today, then they all disappeared."

"Tell me," he said after a moment and plopped himself into a chair. "Who did they actually take away, and who took whom away, and what was all of that anyway that you were talking about?"

"I was visiting here," she said. "I knew someone in Cracow; he was with the American Consulate. I visited him for some time, and then I traveled back. From Cracow to the border is only a short way, but nonetheless my passport disappeared there. I do not believe that I lost it. It could only have been stolen. It was suddenly no longer there, and that was shortly before the border. Instead of calling the Consulate right away, I stupidly tried to cross the border anyway. I was supposed to go to someone in Wiesbaden. I hid in the train. But even though I hid very well, they still found me. I even had the impression that they knew that I had hidden, for the train was stopped for a long time, and they searched for me in the whole train. When I was found I was arrested and brought back to Cracow. I was interrogated but I could state nothing else than that I had lost my passport. I was held there for three weeks and repeatedly interrogated. At the same time they did not even permit me to call either the American or the German Consulate. After that the war started, and I was taken away. That was about ten days ago. But for eight days we have been running on foot. It was horrid. Just look at my shoes!"

And she reached under the bed where her shoes lay next to a pile of clothes. She picked up one of them. It was completely ripped. She looked at it for a moment then let it fall on the floor again.

"It always continued on like that," she added, "day and night. I hardly got any food. You could not even wash. When I came here, I finally had the opportunity to bathe. But that was all. I really do not know where we are here or how I am supposed to get away from here. The Poles are gone, they took everything, I already checked in the closets. I found this dressing gown, but that was just about all. You are the first person that I have seen here. Truly, how did you come here and why do you also not know where we are?"

"This morning," he said, "they took me away, because they believed I was wounded..."

"Is it the wound on your hand?"

"No," he said, "that is from before." And he told her his story. She sat on the bed and looked at him, or rather: she kneeled on the bed, sat on her heels and held her feet in her hands.

"What kind of war is this anyway?" she said. "The Poles seem to be of the opinion they had already lost it."

"It does, at least for now, seem that way," he said.

"Don't you have a cigarette?" she asked.

He arose, walked over to her and offered her a cigarette. "You are a peculiar person," he said as he gave her a light. "Though I do not know you I still find you to be quite a curious person. How could you even attempt to cross the border without a passport? Were you in such a hurry? You said you came from a friend's..."

"Did I say that?" she asked and blushed as she lowered her eyes.

"Yes, roughly."

I was interrogated so often that I formed the habit of being fairly open. I would not have said it otherwise."

"Did you actually then really want to go to a friend in Wiesbaden?"

"No," she laughed and raised her eyes again. "Those were completely different people that I had an appointment with. I was in Cracow too long anyway."

She had completely clear eyes; the white was of complete whiteness. Dark lashes surrounded her stare like rays. She had rose-red lips.

"Every person only has his or her own destiny," he said. "Though one believes that destiny is random, in reality everything that happens to one fits oneself. If you had not come from a friend and had you not – as you said – been on your way to other people, and if you had gone from Cracow to Wiesbaden for some other reasons, all of this would probably not even have happened."

"You think so? Why do you think that?"

The sun had set in the meantime and the room was filled with blue light shining in from the dusk. All things swam in this blue addition to the air, which was more transparent than the air itself. Through the windowpanes the noise resounded in a muffled way from the courtyard, where the livestock was still howling.

"It is true," he said, leaning against the foot of the bed. "And if it were, for example, not my destiny to be here now and even though I do not understand it, nowhere else but here, I would be with a woman now, one whom I have loved, exactly now I would be with her – in order to have this tryst, as people call it. But – even though I have only known this woman for several weeks – she is dead now, and since she assured me of this meeting of ours that we could not have, neither she nor I, I have not seen her again..."

"How do you know that she is not really still alive?" she said. "Or why do you think you know this?"

"Because she was already no longer alive when she promised me this date," he said. "Because she...but you will not understand me. It was someone else who told me that she promised it to me. He obviously did not tell me the truth. Nonetheless, I feel as though she had given it to me herself. I am not there, where I could fulfill it, but believe me, it is the promised time and the promised hour, and it is hard for me to realize that she will not come – only because she cannot come anymore. Generally: some things may be impossible; that something may be impossible in *these* things is immensely hard for the heart to believe."

She was silent, and he added after a short pause:

"But is it not peculiar that we should meet each other here at this time? That I should find you here, so that I would not be alone or so that you would not be alone. Now you know my situation. But I do not know yours, and who even knows about whom you are thinking right now!"

"About no one," she said. "I am listening to you."

"Then you are certainly very forgetful," he said. "But perhaps one should really be forgetful. It does not mean anything when one believes he knows someone, when in reality one does not know him or her. One does not know anyone, least of all oneself, and in theory it does not matter with which memories or fantasies a person surrounds another. After all, people are just people, whether they know one another or not. We are both also like that, you and me, and it is probably the same thing whether we mean others – your someone else or my someone else – or no one. Do you not also believe that?"

He had spoken without looking at her, as if it were not she to whom he had wished to speak. He then reached for her hand and kissed it. She did not answer and when he looked at her she had let her head sink back a bit as if she expected him to also kiss her on her mouth, and with her eyes half-closed she looked at him as with moons. He hesitated for a moment; he had the unclear, obscure idea that actually everything was completely different than he had believed – the reality was: he was a wounded person and she a woman who had been dragged through the entire land. It was the weakness after an immense strain. He leaned over her and kissed her. As she laid her arms around his neck, he saw how they shimmered, rising and lying around him. After that they sank down together.

"It could be," she said, "that you were really not thinking about me. Surely you did not think of me at all – but what type of woman was that whom you were really supposed to meet? What did she look like and what was her name? Can you not tell me since she is, as you told me, no longer alive?"

It had become completely dark in the meantime, and he only saw her as a shimmer, as if starlight lay on her. Everything lay quiet. The disquiet in the courtyard had also stopped. The room became lost in the dark.

"She was very attractive," he said, "almost as attractive as you are and above all very fascinating. But she was not blond, but rather brunette, almost black-haired. She had blue eyes. And also in many other aspects she was quite different from you. I have known you for one hour now – and yet you are here for this meeting that I had with her. But she was like that. Even had she actually been able to come, she might not have come after all. Yes, it could be that she eventually had to die, because she would not have wanted to come after all, to no one... She was like that. It did turn out, though, that she was the divorced wife of a person whose name has nothing to do with this. But she used a different name anyway. She had taken a peculiar name. Her name was Cuba."

He noticed that she pulled herself erect in the dark.

"Cuba?" she said.

"Yes. Cuba Pistohlkors."

She did not answer immediately. "How long have you actually known her?" she asked. "For a few weeks you said? It could only be four weeks, a maximum of five. You have certainly not known her any longer that that. And you said that it was really her you should have met today?"

"Yes," he answered. "Of course. Why do you ask? Did you know her? But that is not possible. You do not know who she really was, and she did have a different name."

"Oh yes," she said. "I know. And also the name is the same. Do you really think you could not find her anymore, and that it was somewhere else that you could have found her? It is certainly only now and here. I am Cuba Pistohlkors."

It was during these days when the campaign in Wolhynien started to come to an end, above all with the battle of Tomaszow and with the surprise attacks that the heroic Colonel Wranja – once one of our own Austrian officers – carried out in the area of Labunie and Zamosc – so that finally even his enemies became proud of him. Wallmoden and Cuba (the real one) remained in Janowka that night, the following day and night. After that they found a team of horses and reached, while constantly changing the team, Liainzut by way of Rawa Ruska and Jaroslau.

The campaign was over on the twenty-third. Summer was also over, and after standing still over the land, a cold wind came, and it even rained this night, after not having rained for twenty-two days; day after day the sun, and night after night the moon and the stars had shone over Poland, over disastrous, beaten, shattered Poland.

On the afternoon of that day, when the starving horses dragged the vehicle through the sand, Wallmoden asked the coachman for the name of the village they were just passing.

"Niwiska," the coachman answered. That was not far from Tarnow. And with his whip he pointed to a village and deserted estate that did not lie far from there. It was, like a thousand others, part village and part estate.

Wallmoden had already been fiddling with his bandage for

some time; he unwound it and Cuba helped him. The wound was exposed. It was already healed.

"Actually," Wallmoden said, after he had looked at her for some time, "actually you have not yet told me where you have this name from – your first name. It is truly unusual. It's a Slavic name, right?" And he threw the bandage out of the vehicle and pulled the glove over his hand.

"Slavic?" she said. "No – it was like this: my father was in the West Indies for many years and he had made himself quite a fortune with a sugar plantation, but returned, rather more perchance than on purpose, shortly before the war – before the last war. After that he married, and when I came into this world, he named me Cuba to remember. Strange, isn't it?"

He was silent, but finally said: "So? I always thought it was Slavic. We have some minor tradesmen whose last name that is. How can you explain that she – I mean: the other – crossed the border with your passport?"

"Oh God," she said, "very easily – I almost crossed the border without a passport. She could have been riding in the sleeping car. You give the passports to the conductor before going to bed, and nobody goes to the trouble to wake the people and to compare their photos."

"Can it still not have been she who stole your passport?"

"No," she said. "Certainly not. It has to have been someone else who did that. I certainly did not see a woman such as you described."

"Too bad," he said. "I mean: for pure interest's sake, too bad. You probably would have liked her except for all of the unpleasantness she caused you. She was peculiar in every respect. She had a certain individuality, one could almost say she was a character. It is strange: I thought about her very much, but now I am beginning to forget her...and yet I cannot forget her. She might have been a person that would not let herself be interrupted by this incident, death, that is, like some other women, of lesser character – more human I mean... Or was it destiny that did not let itself be interrupted? When I was still hoping for this rendezvous, I always secretly feared that she might not want to keep it. But to still keep it..."

He interrupted himself and looked up. The air was suddenly filled with a tremendous roar that filled the entire sky, and even the far areas seemed to swing. Several low flying squadrons of large planes, like dragons, had appeared over the vehicle. They flew slowly. He had not known that they could fly so slowly. It was almost as if they were relaxing for some time during their flight. The campaign was over. They were about to leave Poland. They were flying westwards.

Afterword

One of the most popular Austrian authors of the interwar/postwar periods of the twentieth century, Alexander Lernet-Holenia (1897-1976) has only recently been "rediscovered," and not just for his lingering reputation as an accomplished playwright. So varied is his oeuvre, which includes twenty-five stage plays, twenty-four novels, novellas, short stories, poetry collections, essays, biographies, radio plays and translations, that literary criticism has most preferred to ignore the philosophical and sociopolitical underpinnings of his writings, in order to perpetuate clichés about the author's aristocratic manner, his conservative ideology and his role as the heir to Hugo von Hofmannsthal and Rainer Maria Rilke as one of the final exponents of Viennese literary modernism. While these aspects are not inaccurate, they have for too long detracted from the more precise exploration of a highly sophisticated writer who was not only a great stylist but articulated his own cultural and metaphysical concepts.

Lernet-Holenia's literary roots may be found in *fin de siècle* impressionism, symbolism and aestheticism, but he arrived too late to actually be of those movements, just as he was not of the form-experimental movements that followed. He had found popular fame early, through his dramas and stylish stage comedies, and he was already awarded the prestigious Kleist Prize in 1926. His neo-classical poetry attracted attention in more elite circles, and his prose, particularly the novel on the final days of the Great War and Austria-Hungary's collapse, *Die Standarte* (The Standard, 1934), displayed his immense talent for elegant prose, conversational dialogue, impressionistic beauty and social critique. *Die Standarte* also revealed the author's obsession with the lost Habsburg world – an empire and a polyglot Central European culture he would mourn throughout his life and work. Indeed, Lernet-Holenia's exploration of his own identity (as the son of an aristocratic mother and a mysterious father, he perpetuated the rumor that he was perhaps the natural son of an Austrian archduke) is tightly linked to his reflections on the reinventions of Austrian national and cultural identity. He rejects the new republican world in the interwar period, warning of Nazism at the end of *Die Standarte*, even predicting the destruction of Austria at the hands of Germany and Italy in his allegorical novel *Die Auferstehung des Maltravers* (The Resurrection of Maltravers, 1936), which also parodies Thomas Mann's *Death in Venice* and National Socialist art and literature. Yet, Lernet-Holenia was never an overtly political writer. His interwar prose alternates between the escapism of *Maresi* (1936), *Mona Lisa* (1937), and *Strahlenheim* (1938), and warnings of doom: the Fantastic Realist antiwar novella *Der Baron Bagge* (The Baron Bagge, 1936); the *Nibelungenlied* intertext on German hegemony in Europe in *Der Mann im Hut* (The Man in the Hat, 1937); and the saga of demons and revolution, *Ein Traum in Rot* (A Dream in Red, 1939).

Although he rejected Nazism, he chose to remain in Vienna after the Anschluss, while many of his friends and colleagues went into exile. Having been an imperial officer in the First World War, he easily fell into the role again in the Second, but having been wounded in the attack on Poland, he was transferred to the army's military film office. His work there was limited because he was ideologically suspect (Lernet-Holenia's prose had been "unwelcome" in Germany since 1933). After having provided the basis for what eventually became Germany's greatest film success of the era, the Zarah Leander romance, *Die grosse Liebe* (The Great Love, 1942), he retreated to Vienna, and based on his memories and war diaries, composed the novel *Mars im Widder* (Mars in Aries) between December 15, 1939 and February 15, 1940. The novel first appeared uncensored and in serialized form in the magazine *Die Dame* (The Lady) that same year. The Ministry of Propaganda, which even confiscated the customary author's copies, immediately forbade the 15,000 copies of the novel printed by S. Fischer Publishers in 1941. The entire stock, housed in a Leipzig warehouse, was destroyed in an Allied air raid, but Lernet-Holenia managed to republish the novel from a rediscovered proof copy found in Stockholm in 1947. The actual subversive messages of the novel were not understood by Goebbels, who rejected the work primarily due to its overt respect for the Poles and for its less than typical hero. The novel's lack of support for Nazi racial doctrine and a heroic war had additional consequences: Lernet-Holenia's plays were no longer performed and his earlier books would not be reprinted. In 1942, he expanded the fragment chapter "Silverstolpe," which he wrote around 1924, into his second and final novel of the war period, *Beide Sizilien* (Two Sicilies). Disguised as a detective novel with a contrived plot featuring numerous assumed identities and set in 1925 Vienna, this monument to a lost Austria is only slightly less subversive than the previous novel. It is considered by many critics to be one of Lernet-Holenia's most successful works. Hilde Spiel equates portions of the novel with Hofmannsthal's *The Letter of Lord Chandos* and Proust's *Remembrances of Things Past* and according to Paul Kruntorad it remains "one of the most beautifully written novels in Austrian literature." Missing the point completely, the Propaganda Ministry approved publication, obviously considering it a safe foray into the nostalgia of drawing-room mystery, a mild recant of the insolence of *Mars im Widder*.

Lernet-Holenia was able to continue his work and fame in the postwar era when many had interrupted their careers with exile and political taint. In fact, the author was so popular that in 1948 Austrian critic Hans Weigel remarked that Austrian literature now only consisted of two authors – Lernet and Holenia. An ironic assertion indeed, given the dualism surrounding the author and the themes of his work. Lernet-Holenia immediately took on the Nazi past, when other Austrian writers tended to avoid this subject, in such provocative works as the novella, *Der 20. Juli* (The 20th of July, 1946) and the long-poem *Germanien* (1946). Several adventure and social satire novels followed, but the author also produced two of the most fascinating novels on personal and national guilt in the postwar era: *Der Graf von Saint-Germain* (The Count of Saint-Germain, 1948) which focused on elitism, apathy and the Anschluss, and *Der Graf Luna* (The Count Luna, 1955), a jaundiced look at postwar Austria though the destructive paranoia of a man unable to resolve his guilt of having unintentionally sentenced a man to death in a concentration camp. His prose turned to various subjects in the 1960s and 70s, ranging from accomplished historical biographies (*Prinz Eugen*, 1960) and historical novels (*Das Halsband der Königin*/The Queen's Necklace, 1962), to short story collections (*Götter und Menschen*/Gods and Men, 1964); philosophical/ metaphysical novels (*Pilatus: Ein Komplex*/Pilatus: A Complex, 1967; *Die Beschwörung*/The Conjuring, 1974) and metaphorical explorations of personal and national identity (*Vitrine XIII*/Cabinet XIII, 1966; *Die Hexen*/The Witches, 1969; *Die Geheimnisse des Hauses Österreich*/The Secrets of the House of Austria, 1971).

Lernet-Holenia remained outside of literary trends and his topics continued to be more oriented towards the past than to the future. In the youth-led cultural movements of the 1960s and 70s this was certain artistic death. Nevertheless, he continued to criticize Austrian and German society, politics and culture, rejecting artistic revolution for its own sake, recalling the value of "nobility" and high-culture in life, and managing to make a cause celebre out of his resignation from the presidency of the Austrian P.E.N. club in a vague protest of Heinrich Böll's Nobel Prize. Ultimately, as the author's notions of an aristocratic world-view lost resonance in popular thought and his eccentric personality overshadowed his literary fame, much of his work fell into obscurity. The new interest in Alexander Lernet-Holenia since the late 1990s, particularly in Austria, may be the result of an increased national discourse on the past and on national identity, on the emergence of postmodernism, or on the influence of the work by Austrianists outside of the country. Whatever the reasons, the return of Lernet-Holenia's wide-ranging work to the canon is not only deserving but necessary – for its stylistic accomplishment, its "unofficial" history of the Austrian and Central European experience in the twentieth century, its exploration and critique of Austrian identity, history and culture, and its unique philosophical prowess. The masterwork of *Mars in Aries* makes this very clear.

The two distinct halves of *Mars in Aries* – the home front (Vienna) and the battle front (Poland) mirror each other in the threats to and alienation of the central character, Wallmoden, an Austrian aristocrat called up for duty as an officer in the German army. Even without the too-human image of Poland which doomed the book to censorship in 1941, the very notion that there was no enthusiasm for the war at home subverts the Nazi dictum of a satisfied Aryan world and popular support for its military action. One of the few overt elements of resistance to the German New Order in the novel is the specific Old Austrian nature of the characters, for the most part Viennese aristocrats who do not even pay lip service to German cultural or political hegemony of their city. With the introduction of the mysterious circle of Herr von Oertel and Baron Drska, and the central figure of Cuba von Pistohlkors, it is impossible not to surmise that some form of organized Austrian/Central European irredentism against National Socialism is at work in the novel. *Mars in Aries* is richly constructed with cultural, historical, literary, linguistic, philosophical and metaphysical references that counter Nazism and expose the premeditation behind the attack on Poland.

The events of Count Wallmoden's life relating to his love affair with Cuba, serves as an excuse to reveal the planning and calculation of the attack on Poland on September 1, 1939. The novel's timeline begins with what seems the arbitrary date of Wallmoden's report for a routine maneuver – August 15, 1939 – and continues as the attack is planned and executed. The deception surrounding the German designs on Poland – the secret protocol for the country's division in the German-Soviet Non-Aggression Pact and the German fabrication of Polish aggression in the staging of an attack on a German radio station in Gleiwitz on August 31, 1939 – is echoed in Cuba's deception, the deception of her circle, and the false messages of Wallmoden's attempt to reach Cuba from the battlefront: although he sends her a telegram, she may never have received it. Rex first informs him that he did see Cuba in Vienna, then admits he did not. With the introduction of Cuba and her mysterious actions in Vienna, the author seasons the novel with numerous clues via names and locations which are codes for Austrian identity and culture, or elements of Catholic or humanist history. A few examples: upon leaving the Sodoma apartment, Wallmoden drives Cuba to the Salesianergasse. The Salesians, named after the seventeenth-century Bishop Francis de Sales, were members of a Catholic order founded in Turin in 1845. It was founded to administer education, instruction, and Catholic missionary work. Cuba is linked with this street throughout the novel, as if she were a member of the order. Wallmoden first thinks that he will have to deliver Cuba's letter to Rodaun or Heiligenstadt. Both towns are symbolic of Austrian culture and identity: Rodaun was the home of Hugo von Hofmannsthal, the originator of the conservative Austrian Idea; Heiligenstadt conveys connections with Catholic theology. Now a district of Vienna, it skirts the Kahlenberg, an important site in the Christian victory over the second Turkish siege of Vienna in 1683. Oertel's home is on the Piaristengasse, named after a Catholic teaching order founded in Austria and Poland in 1607. This street is repeatedly mentioned throughout the novel, in connection with Cuba's friends.

With its astrological title, Lernet-Holenia casts a metaphysical/ fatalistic setting over the action, and the novel incorporates the author's customary foray into the fantastic, into the dream world. The visions here appear to be a product of Wallmoden's confusion, his inability to fathom the secrets of Cuba's world, and the surrealism of the wanton destruction of Poland. Moreover, the mysticism of the novel arises from the mystery, power and seemingly inescapable course of nature. The astral prediction of war – the position of the planet Mars in the Aries constellation – and the prediction of catastrophe in the signs of nature are symptomatic of Lernet-Holenia's fatalism. The apocalyptic feeling which pervades the novel is brought about by the insistence that fate ultimately subverts and controls both the National Socialist hegemony as well as Wallmoden's life and the actions of the Cuba/ Oertel resistance group. The red star that appears in the night sky is soon joined by "a glassy glint, like the eye of a madman: Saturn had risen above the horizon" – the possible indication of the two forces that will seal the fate of Poland, Stalin and Hitler. While fishing for crayfish with toads as bait, Wallmoden recalls how the toads refused to move and "remained in the right" even after they were slain - "the broad sitting-there of a mass." Clearly, Lernet-Holenia suggests Gandhi's notion of peaceful resistance by the victimized Poles.

The haunting western migration of the crayfish over land, has been variously understood to symbolize the approach of Soviet tanks, the exodus of Poles fleeing from the Nazi/Soviet aggression, even the Holocaust. Wallmoden's responds to this vision by quoting a scene from the Apocalypse – in the Latin Vulgate rather than in the Protestant German version. Indeed, the most prominent feature of *Mars in Aries*, which counters the National Socialist anti-*langue* visual ideology is its concentration on the value of books and the word itself. Wallmoden finds spiritual direction in the found volume of poetry, the book itself symbolizing the vast European culture that National Socialism threatens. Rosthorn's explanations and admonitions in Latin, which interrupt the German narrative, do far more than equate German hegemony with the barbarism of the Roman Empire; they subvert the National Socialist beatification of German "race" and language as the ultimate culture. Rosthorn's discourse implies a different German historical experience, a humanist, albeit an essentially elitist one: it is a specifically Catholic Austrian *langue*, which, in Rosthorn's Latin commentary on Roman folly, negates fascist images of German racial and military superiority.

The false Cuba, who explains herself as an adventuress and who remains largely undefined, is the author's strongest expression of female equality with the heroic male figures of his oeuvre. Nevertheless, Oertel's and Wallmoden's auratization of female beauty by comparison with classical sculpture, which the male gaze deconstructs into object parts – legs, eyes, hair, skin, and breasts – stresses the author's reticence, much of it stemming from his influence by symbolist/impressionist literature, to create a realistic female character. This remains so despite his obvious attempts to break the myth of female inferiority here and in *Der Baron Bagge*. Oertel's description of her purity and decency evokes the icon of the Christian virgin. But more importantly, Cuba also represents the "beautiful soul" of Goethe, who in her platonic love and ideal beauty (the comparisons with classical images) redeems the male from a life of ugliness. The true Cuba also does this in the evocation of love as Eros (again evoking comparisons with classical images) as she stands naked and again rescues Wallmoden from the ugliness of his immediate war experiences.

References to an Old Europe now at odds with contemporary National Socialist reality are frequent in Wallmoden's and Cuba's long-winded conversations. Since her identity is false, the reader cannot know if her autobiographical statements are pure fantasy or elements from her true identity. The author, however, offers interesting clues as to her nonconformist, even subversive nature. She proudly explains that her name is actually a Czech name. In response to Wallmoden's statement that the Pistohlkors are Balts, Cuba comments that he nevertheless had a German passport, suggesting the eradication of national identity by pan-German National Socialism. Cuba also mentions that she was engaged in Santa Monica, California, the well-known enclave of German cultural figures in exile, as well as the beneficial "climate" her actor husband found there.

Rivers, bridges, and underground passages are common to Lernet-Holenia's fiction. They are his pathways into self-realization or self-loss; transit points from one realm of reality into another, from life to death, from current existence into an existence yet to come. On the journey to Poland, the Danube, which seems to already mourn the approaching warriors, evokes the doomed crossing in the *Nibelungenlied* epic. It also recalls the slaughter on the Danube bridge in *Die Standarte*, the author's metaphor for the destruction of *Mitteleuropa*. Like the many other oppositions in the novel, the interplay of dust and water are important symbols of life and death: the two bathing women and their wet footprints on the ground; the traces of the wet footprints of the real Cuba (named after an island – a land mass surrounded by water) in the dusty Polish manor house; the soldier's sleeping faces covered with dust appear to Wallmoden as if they are frozen in snow – prefiguring the fate of the army on the Eastern Front.

The Venetian Song also fits into this dust/water interplay and suggests the "shores" of perception, which mark the transition between consciousness and unconsciousness. Inner Emigration poet Rudolf Hagelstange, known for his poetry cycle *Venezianisches Credo* (Venetian Credo), symbolized Venice as an island of freedom and peace. The prose poem Wallmoden discovers instructs him to find sleep there – an admonition to escape from the horrors of reality into a twilight world, a realm where escape or even change is possible. And it is in the twilight that he finally meets the true Cuba.

Lernet-Holenia's anxieties regarding his own origin/identity and his notion of a phantom imperial Austria (the sociocultural ideal of the lost Habsburgian Central Europe) beyond the Austrian republic foster a sense of dualism in his writings. His characters assume new identities and reputations, or are mistaken for other characters. There is even a gender crossing and a "resurrection." In *Mars in Aries*, Wallmoden often feels he is split into two people in two distinct places, there is the notion of spiriting, of ghosts and the many shadows that appear represent a doubling of the physical presence. Moreover, characters have double identities or reputations. This doubling relates to a third pole in a Platonic two-three scheme of existence. The structure extends across all thematic levels of the novel and is the key to the work's subversive quality. Each theme also extends to three realms – the personal, the social, and the political. Following the two-three pattern, the author makes the first two explicit, which comment on a third one (political), which remains implicit. Even the resistance aspects follow this pattern: the false Cuba resists Wallmoden sexually, the officers consider the Polish resistance against their aggression, and both are a comment on the unspoken political resistance of Cuba, Oertel and their group.

The interplay of fate and will sets the relationships between self, world, and a divine force. Wallmoden emerges from a communal world he cannot identify with (like the author -- as an aristocrat in a mass culture and an Old Austrian/*Mitteleuropean* in a pan-German *Reich*) into individual realization, and finally into the universal, through the false Cuba's platonic love. Lernet-Holenia also evokes Ernst Mach in the novel's emphasis of sensation over understanding, and Kant in the suggestion that one can never see things as they really are – we can only know them by their effects. Lernet-Holenia states in his foreword to the 1947 edition of the novel, the 1941 "preprint drew so much attention, not only in Germany, but also with the troops in the field (if in fact it was read the way I meant it to be)..." His hope was that the reader, numbed by official (dis)information, would locate the implicit meanings, would understand the "effects" in the novel and trust sensations and effects in their own lives as a pathway to the truth.

The value of Lernet-Holenia's *Mars in Aries* to today's readership extends far beyond its literary brilliance. As a cultural document, it evokes concepts that span the classical and European cultural heritage. As the unofficial history of a time and place – of a war - it is both richly specific and universal. As a presentation of an author's worldview, it is nothing less than the suggestion that art might still change our lives.

Robert von Dassanowsky